Dreaming out Loud

A Collection of "If..."
Tales from the Imagination

Kevin Creager

Black Rose Writing | Texas

The author grants the final approval for this literary material.

First printing

This is a work of fiction. Names, characters, businesses, places, events, and incidents are either the products of the author's imagination or used in a fictitious manner. Any resemblance to actual persons, living or dead, or actual events is purely coincidental.

ISBN: 978-1-68513-348-1
LIBRARY OF CONGRESS CONTROL NUMBER: 2023942551
PUBLISHED BY BLACK ROSE WRITING
www.blackrosewriting.com

Printed in the United States of America
Suggested Retail Price (SRP) $19.95

Dreaming Out Loud is printed in Garamond Premier Pro

*As a planet-friendly publisher, Black Rose Writing does its best to eliminate unnecessary waste to reduce paper usage and energy costs, while never compromising the reading experience. As a result, the final word count vs. page count may not meet common expectations.

PRAISE FOR
KEVIN CREAGER

In 2017, *We Cuss a Little: The Life and Times of a School Psychologist*, was named one of the nine essential books for a school psychologist's bookshelf.

In January 2020, *The Body on the Roof* was awarded the Pencraft Award for Literary Excellence as Second Place in Mysteries. It was called "A well-crafted debut novel..." by Connie Chappell, author of *Lily White Lie, A Wrenn Grayson Mystery*.

"What is shown to us each time is an idea, a little piece of speculative universe, and we peek into it..." –Russell Meredith, author of *The Psychic Battery*

This book is dedicated to my wife, Sue, who has had to put up with my spending so many hours 'playing' at the computer, when I could have been doing something much more useful, my children – Colin (Katie), Alex (Hannah), Laura (Greg), and my grandchildren – Colette, Emily, Alanna, Riley, and Cameron, for whom many of these stories have been imagined, fanciful or not.

Special thanks and acknowledgements to the Springfield Writers' Club, for their feedback on the many rough first drafts, and to the many friends and family who have willingly served as readers and critiquers. It has been greatly appreciated.

Dreaming out Loud

If ... you find yourself with some spare time on a drive along a coast, any coast, and you spot a lonely stone church up on a hillside, maybe you'd like to visit the inside of the church, just to see what it's like. Or maybe you'd rather not ...

IN TIME

Jimmy Goodrich rolled down the car window and let the early morning chill hit him full in the face. He shook his head to lose the remaining cobwebs and started singing along with the Rolling Stones on the radio.

It had been a long, hard winter of work, and Jimmy was taking a brief vacation break, looking forward to some time to himself. Driving along the Maine coastline usually lent itself to stream-of-consciousness thinking, and this trip was no exception. For the first time in several months, he didn't have to be anywhere in particular, didn't have to do anything in particular, and, most importantly, didn't have to think of anything in particular.

Jimmy stopped where he felt like stopping, ate when and where he felt like eating, and did whatever he felt like doing. He was willing to let himself lose track of time and space – anything to get away from thoughts of his job.

It was probably still mid-morning when he first spotted the little stone church alone on the distant hillside. He was somewhere between Hanport and Bellport, or between Stannetport and Pundleport. He really hadn't kept track, and he had seen no towns and little traffic since rising.

Pulling over alongside the road, he took out the camera that he still liked to use on trips, and snapped a few pictures of the morning sun lighting the stained-glass windows. Though it was a distance away, he had a sudden impulse to see the inside, and he was still very much in the mood to act on those impulses.

It took some time to find the narrow road that led to it, and, if there had been any schedule to keep, he wouldn't have bothered. The last stretch was more of a dirt track than anything else. About a quarter of a mile from the church, he passed a young woman standing beside the road. He was going slow enough to wave, and he thought she nodded in reply. Her head turned to watch the car, and he noticed in his rearview mirror that, after he had passed, she started to walk in the same direction.

There were only two vehicles parked in front of the church –- a battered pickup of indeterminate age, and a small compact car that also looked as if it had seen a few years.

He pulled in behind them, slung his camera over his shoulder, and wandered over to read the name carved over the front door. St. Martha's Church of the Lost Souls. He grinned, thinking that about covered him right now.

He pulled the front, the one and only, door open and stepped inside. It took a moment for his eyes to adjust to the darkness, but he immediately realized that he must have interrupted a service as a voice reading scripture abruptly stopped for a few seconds, then continued.

Another voice whispered to him from the shadows to the right.

"Do not worry. Reverend Bentner is not used to interruptions, particularly from someone unfamiliar, and, even more specifically, in this church."

Jimmy turned and by now could make out an older man wearing a cleric's collar.

"I'm sorry. I didn't realize there was a service going on." He also whispered.

The cleric chuckled.

"Well, as they be, there have not been many of those here lately, that is for certain." He pointed into the sanctuary. "Why do you not take a seat in a pew? This will not go on much longer."

As Jimmy sat down, he realized there were only about six or seven others sitting. They were all in the first two pews, which left him about six pews back, in the last one. At the front of the church, the minister had finished reading and was now dripping water onto a baby held by its mother. A man stood next to her, nervously twisting a hat in his hands. Jimmy realized he had walked in on a baptism.

The door behind him creaked open again, but this time the minister did not pause. Jimmy turned and saw that the young woman from the road had entered. The other cleric was not in sight and, after a few seconds, she came forward and stood next to his pew. He slid over and she sat down.

She leaned toward him and whispered, "Do you know who they're baptizing?"

Jimmy shrugged. "No, I just got here. Don't you?"

She stared ahead for a few more seconds, then turned to him and shook her head. "I just felt like I should come in. That I needed to be in here."

The ceremony finished, and the mother beamed at the minister. The father breathed a sigh of apparent relief and started to put his hat on, then realized he was still in church and awkwardly passed it back and forth between his hands. Those in the pews stood up and circled the couple and the baby, making the usual sorts of comments.

"Oh, he was so good ..."

"Look, he's smiling now. I bet he knows what's happening ..."

"Do you think he looks like the mother or the father?"

They slowly parted as the baby's parents walked down the aisle and out the door, but the congregation stayed where they were, then looked toward Jimmy.

The minister who had performed the baptism started down the aisle, and Jimmy and the young woman stood. Stopping next to their pew, the minister held out his hand.

"Hello, I'm Reverend Bentner. It was nice to have you with us. Is there anything that I can do to help you?"

"We just stopped in to see the church." Jimmy noticed that the woman had moved toward the group at the front. "I'm sorry. I didn't mean to interrupt anything. I was just passing by, and, ... just felt like coming in."

"Well, I'm very happy to hear that. It's nice to know the church can still pull them in occasionally. That sort of thing doesn't happen as often as it used to."

He looked around the sanctuary. "There aren't too many people that use this church anymore. I don't think there ever were very many, but at least they were regular. Now, I'm lucky if I get three for a service. For example," he waved his hand at the door, "that father hasn't been in here since their wedding. And the mother only comes to bring in her grandmother about once a month."

"That doesn't sound like enough to keep the church open, if you don't mind my saying so."

Reverend Bentner chuckled, but with little humor.

"Actually, I serve five churches, all like this one. But this is the smallest. If these churches weren't here, there wouldn't be anywhere for these people to go. There isn't enough money among them to build a church for them all, and they're not going to attend one of the others."

Jimmy became aware that the others were still standing at the front, maybe whispering a little among themselves, but focusing most of their attention upon himself and the preacher. He faced the minister again.

"I guess that does keep you busy. So tell me, just how old is this building?"

"The building itself is about 180 years old. But most of the inside was destroyed in a fire about 150 years ago and was gradually replaced over the next thirty to forty years. There has been little change since then. Except for less and less people coming. But then some of that may be attributed to the stories about the fire."

"Oh?" Despite it just having been a polite question, Jimmy found his wandering attention snap back to the answer.

"Local legend has it that the fire was the work of the devil. Of course, anything bad that happens in a church is rumored to be the work of the devil." The minister led him to near the door. "Apparently, the fire broke out in this area during a service. Most of the congregation escaped, but some didn't. By the time they were able to get anything organized to combat the fire, the church was gutted and the people inside were dead." He shook his head. "The fire was in front of the only door, but it's always been puzzling as to how it got so big so fast that they couldn't put it out, and how most people got out safely, but some didn't. So, it was either the work of the devil tormenting the good or the work of God punishing the bad. Take your pick. I won't. I'm not arrogant enough to believe I can discern God's will when it comes to people dying."

Jimmy ran his hand along the stone wall. "It must have taken some time to restore it so it could be used again."

"Yes, it did. Actually, it took longer than it needed to, as many locals wouldn't come near the place afterward. In fact, a good many of their descendants still consider the place cursed and some even think it is haunted."

"I'm surprised it's still open, then."

The minister shrugged. "There are always some people who go to church, whatever the situation. And, to be honest, most of the ones that attend come only because they have always lived near here and this has always been their church. I guess they feel bound to this area in some way."

He reached for the door and pulled it open.

"I'm afraid I have a hospital visit to make. You're welcome to stay and look around, or sit and contemplate. We never lock the door, so don't worry about that. I expect you won't be disturbed while you're here."

Jimmy shook his hand again. "Thank you very much. I appreciate your time, but I'll probably be leaving myself in a few minutes."

As soon as the door closed behind Reverend Bentner, a voice spoke at Jimmy's shoulder.

"So, as you be, what did you think of the story of the fire?"

Startled, Jimmy turned to find the man with the clerical collar that had first met him at the door. The man chuckled and held his hand up.

"I am sorry. I did not mean to frighten you."

"That's alright. I'm afraid I'd forgotten you were here. I didn't see you after the baptism."

Jimmy looked toward the front of the church and discovered that the same small group of people were still there and were still looking at him. Engrossed in the fire story, he had forgotten them, too.

"Oh, you still have something going on. I didn't realize that. I'll just be leaving..."

"Now, now, you are not interrupting anything." The man walked toward the group and it forced Jimmy to follow to keep listening. "I am Father

McCahu, and we have another story which I believe may be of interest to you."

Father McCahu put his hand on the altar and turned to face Jimmy. The others sat down where they were, but the young woman walked to the side and stood against the wall.

Jimmy tried again. "Look, I'm sorry. I just stopped to see the church. It's a nice church, but it's time for me to be going and I don't want to hold you up from whatever you're doing. These other people are obviously here for something."

"You have noted the other people, then?"

"Yeah," Jimmy was surprised at the comment, they were right there. "I thought they were here for the baptism, but apparently also for something else."

"They are here for everything."

The cleric rubbed his hand along the smooth top of the altar. The gesture displayed affection and a habit of long standing. He looked back at Jimmy.

"What is astounding is that you are aware of them. And of me."

Jimmy shifted in confusion, "Well, it's not a very big church…"

"You misunderstand me." Father McCahu held up his hand. "What I mean, as I be, is no one else has seen us … in one hundred and fifty years."

The silence would have been deafening if Jimmy had paid any attention to it. The young woman straightened up and took two steps away from the wall. Jimmy turned, and for the first time, looked closely at the others.

The young woman he had noticed before. Two elderly women held handbags in their laps and glanced at each other. A seven- or eight-year-old boy sat between what apparently were his mother and father, who squeezed hands along the pew above his head. A middle-aged man ran a finger along the lapel of his coat. The clothing did look old-fashioned, but Jimmy had simply thought it appropriate for the out-of-the-way mountains. They all seemed to be waiting, to be expecting something from him.

"You do not believe me, do you?"

"I, … I don't know what you're saying."

The cleric stepped down and put his hand on Jimmy's shoulder.

"To be simply put, we are ghosts. Spirits rather."

"No, you're not." It was an automatic statement, with no thought or intent behind it.

Father McCahu chose to laugh. "Yes, we are. We have been this way for so long that I am afraid we could not anticipate how someone would react. The fact that you are still here speaks much of you."

"But I can touch you. I can feel you touch me. And talk to you. And see you. Why can I do this if no one else has for one hundred and fifty years?"

Jimmy stepped away from the Father and peered up into the corners of the sanctuary.

"What is this? Is this some kind of joke? Am I on Candid Camera or something?"

The cleric looked blank for a moment. "I know that to be candid is to be truthful, and, through the years we have learned what a camera is. It is a device, such as what you have over your shoulder, that visitors point at an object and an image of the object appears on paper. Do you mean that this image cannot lie? But why would you be on a candid camera?"

"That's it! I'm going to take a picture of you." Jimmy unslung his camera and took first a picture of the cleric, then one of the group sitting in the pews, and finally one of the girl near the wall. "There, if you're ghosts, you shouldn't show up on film, should you?

Father McCahu shrugged. "I do not know. I have no experience in these matters. What does your camera tell you?"

Jimmy held up the back of his camera and moved next to the Father to show him the picture. Of the inside of the church.

Nothing else, just the altar and the walls. No cleric. He forwarded to the next shot. Same thing. No people.

"Ok, now I'm getting freaked out."

Father McCahu shrugged again. It was a slight shrug, but one meant to convey, "I don't know what to tell you."

"Reverend Bentner told you about the fire. We are the ones who perished at that time. But we have never left.

"The fire was to the left of the door at first, which is why so many were able to exit safely. But it spread quickly, blocking our only way out. Mabel and Bertha always sit in the front pew, so were furthest from the door. Peter," McCahu pointed to the boy, "had fallen asleep, and it took a moment to rouse him. I, of course, was in front and was not leaving until everyone else had. John was ensuring that 'women and children first' was being followed, then came back for Bertha and Mabel. By that time, the fire had completely blocked the door.

"And we have not been able to leave since."

Jimmy was lost in the story, but spotted a small door behind the altar and raised his hand to point.

Father McCahu turned to look.

"Yes, that door, as it is, is here, now. It was put in place when they rebuilt the church. But it has not been opened since. As there has been no call for it."

Jimmy shook his head as if to awaken.

"Can't you leave? Can't you walk through the door now? Or go wherever it is that ... dead people go? No offense."

"We are here. Why, I do not know. Maybe we need help. We have tried to walk out the door, but have been ... stopped. I don't know how else to put it. We follow people leaving, but cannot penetrate that opening."

Jimmy turned to the young woman. "You were outside, down the road. I saw you. How did you get there?" He turned back to the Father. "You didn't mention her."

McCahu looked puzzled. "She is not one of us. We thought she came with you."

"What? No! I passed her on the road as I drove here. I've never seen her before!"

"She came in and sat with you."

"I'm friendly! I didn't know her. She just came and sat with me!" He turned to her, but paused and looked at his camera, fingering the shots over one more. Yes, she was there in that last one.

"Why are you here? And, can you see them?" He swept his arm toward the others.

She looked startled. But then, Jimmy had not been paying attention to her throughout the story, so she may have looked that way all along.

"Yes, I can see them. And it's scaring me that I can." She drew a deep breath. "My name is Julie Bannock. I don't know why I am here. I am from Michigan, but I was drawn to this area. It just felt like I had to be here today. I was hiking from Brookport, just knowing that I had to go somewhere when you passed me, and I saw the church and knew this is where I needed to be."

"So, you and I are real?" Jimmy walked over to her and touched her arm, simply to reassure himself. "Just us?"

The mother and father stirred, and the father spoke for the first time.

"Bannock? Our name is Bannock. I had a brother who moved west, to Ohio, I think, but he could have gone on to Michigan. His name was Jonas Bannock. Does that ring a bell?"

"I, I don't know." Julie was slow to respond. "My great-grandfather was Randall, but I don't know beyond that. Do you think that's why I'm here? Because we're both Bannocks?"

The father licked his lips. "My name is Randall. It may be a coincidence, but I suspect it is more than that."

Father McCahu held up his hand. "There must be a reason. For many events in this world, there is not. But you are both here and you are the first that have been able to interact with us. There must be a reason."

He looked at the door and walked to it.

"This is where we have been stopped so many times. I said perhaps we needed assistance to cross this threshold. And perhaps," he looked at Jimmy and Julie, "you are the ones to help us."

"Randall, Mary, Peter, come here. Julie, if you are truly meant to be here, come here and take Mary's hand."

He touched each of them with affection and said, "May God bless you. Now, go."

Julie walked through the door, and the family passed with her. They were gone from the church.

Everyone that was left looked at each other.

Father McCahu smiled at Jimmy. "Your name wouldn't be McCahu, would it?"

"No, no. My name is Jimmy, James, Goodrich."

There was a sudden intake of breath from both Mabel and Bertha, and Bertha (or it could have been Mabel) said, "Our sister, Vera, married a Goodrich, Laurence Goodrich."

"That was my great, great-grandparents' names. Vera and Larry. Maybe, maybe I am here for you."

The Father nodded. "That could be, that could very well be."

He went to each of the sisters and touched them. "God bless you both."

Jimmy reached out his hand to take Mabel's (or Bertha's) and they walked through the door.

On the other side, he let go of Bertha (or Mabel). They both smiled at him, then were gone.

Julie was still standing, as if waiting for him.

"The same thing happened to my family. They didn't go back inside, did they?"

Jimmy shook his head. "No, they didn't return." He took his own deep breath. "They are gone. But the pastor and the other man were still there. I'm going back in to see what happens now."

They both reentered the church, with a little more wariness than before. Father McCahu and John were standing just inside.

The Father raised an eyebrow.

"They disappeared as soon as we let go their hands." Jimmy peered around the church. "They didn't come back, did they?"

"No, I think they have left for good." He looked at John.

"My name is Smith." His eyes passed from Jimmy to Julie, but without any real hope. "That's unlikely to be helpful here. And I know I was not related to the others, so doubtful any kinship to either of you."

"John," McCahu spoke directly to him. "I know it was of great concern to you that the congregation get safely out of the church during the fire and that you were greatly distressed for those who did perish. But you have spoken very little throughout the years, and never about yourself. You were not a regular member here. In fact, the day of the fire was your first time in the church, I believe."

"That is right, Father."

"So, perhaps, as it be, your leaving may have somewhat to do with why you were here that day."

John sighed deeply. Soul-searingly deeply, and looked at the floor. He eventually raised his head to look the Father straight in the eye.

"I started the fire."

"I know." McCahu's response was so soft to be barely audible. "I never raised the issue in front of the others, but I always knew."

"I was hired by a man, it certainly doesn't matter who now, to burn down buildings in this area, because he wanted the land. There was no intent for anyone to die, but he thought no one would return to the church once it had been burned out." He grasped McCahu by the shoulders.

"I swear to you, Father, in front of God Almighty! No one was supposed to die! I did my best to get them out, but, when I saw some weren't going to make it, I knew I had to stay too."

Father McCahu reached up and held the top of Smith's head.

"You are forgiven. You have paid your penance. May God bless you."

He turned to Jimmy and Julie.

"Thank you. You will never know the peace you have brought to this place, but thank you. And may God bless your lives."

Taking John Smith by the arm, the two of them walked through the door and disappeared into the day.

Turning to Julie, Jimmy said, "Did this really happen? Were they really here?" He looked back at the altar area. "It really feels empty now. I don't think I will be back here again."

Julie smiled, a warm, happy smile.

"You are here, and I am here, and something happened. But, yes, I am ready to leave now."

Taking Jimmy's hand, just in case, they walked out the door.

I WANDER ON

I wander on
Until the morning sun is gone
Until the day's events have finally passed.

There's more to life
Than we can ever ponder on
So let us live today and make our memories last.

We raise a toast
To those we've loved and those we've known
To those still here and those who've gone
We raise a toast
To another dawn.

If... you are a male, and, hopefully, some of you are, and you are sent on a shopping errand by your wife with a very important shopping list, that you somehow happen to misplace, what do you do? Do you return home and admit your mistake, or do you plunge ahead and buy everything you can possibly think of?

A MALE'S ADVENTURES IN SHOPPING

As soon as he slipped through the sliding door of the Jumbomart Supermegastore, Sam realized he had made a mistake.

A big mistake.

He had forgotten his shopping list. He looked in his right pocket, then his left pocket, then his back right pocket, then his back left pocket, then the funny pockets down close to his knees. Nothing.

And the last thing that Junie, his dear, beloved, exasperated wife, had said to him before he left home was, "Don't forget the list before you leave home." And he had nodded, as husbands do, and not really thought about what she had said until just now. So going home twenty miles to retrieve it was out of the question.

Sneaking home maybe, but not simply going home.

And no cell phone, which had been left behind precisely so Junie couldn't call with additional, "necessary" items.

He looked around vaguely. With a list, he had stood a chance of getting through the store by heading only to certain departments. Without a list and in a smaller, regular, normal store, he stood a chance of getting through it by going aisle to aisle, and letting visual stimuli jog his memory.

But here? With acres and acres, miles and miles, aisle after aisle after aisle after...?

"Here you are, sir." An elderly gentleman wearing a pink vest with "Gerald" on the name tag was slowly, almost visibly, pushing a cart in his direction. He reached out to take the cart, as much to keep Gerald from having to push the cart any further as to take it to use. The poor guy was already wheezing and needed to lean against a post to catch his breath, before heading the few feet back to the cart stand for another one. Sam looked down at the cart. Apparently, he was committed now. He didn't really want to have Gerald go to the trouble of taking it back to the stand.

He slowly began walking in the direction that the cart was already facing, to the far right of the store. Sam thought he might as well start using the aisle-by-aisle method and see how far he got. He didn't look behind him to see how far he did have to get. That sort of goal was bound to be self-defeating.

A frantic woman with two young noisy children in her cart, and three not-quite-so-young noisy kids hanging on to her legs and the sides of the cart pushed by him. The sounds of "Mommy, can we get some...?" actually seemed to get louder as the family moved further away. He slowed a little more to let the distance grow, but was bumped from behind.

"Excuse me, but can I get to the tanning lotion?"

He glanced over to see an older woman, old enough to be his grandmother, or maybe even his grandmother's grandmother, gesturing to the display next to him. He realized he was blocking her reach, muttered, "I'm sorry", and resumed pushing the cart.

It seemed a long way even to this end of the store. *Whoever had first thought that a store this big was a good idea?* And he hadn't even started yet. Along the front were apparently the seasonal displays – such as the tanning lotions, swim fins, small surf boards (*for what? There wasn't an ocean for thousands of miles*), small wading pools (*must be for the small surf boards*), beach towels, beach chairs, and so on and so on. And it was March. Come summer, Sam realized, these items would no longer be considered seasonal and he would see rows of jackets and back-to-school supplies. Commercial establishments always seemed to be anticipating potential consumer wants, but not addressing their urgent, immediate needs.

This wasn't helping. Nothing in the cart and nothing coming to mind. Sam was tempted to grab a towel just to have something in the cart. He gave in to temptation and started looking through a colorful pile of them. Didn't want a big fish, or a sand castle, or a bikini-clad female (well..., but he was going to be in enough trouble with Junie). He finally found one that was just bright colored stripes and thought that it would do.

Now, he had actually started shopping. On to the next department.

Which happened to be shoes. Sam didn't remember shoes on the list, but was there anything else – shoe laces, slippers, insoles?

"Excuse me, but can I get to the shoe polish?"

Surprised, Sam recognized his grandmother's grandmother again. "Sure, sorry." He pushed his cart slowly onward, but slowed again when he heard loud familiar voices from the next aisle – "Mommy, can we get...?" *What could they possibly be whining about in the shoes?*

He at least thought he should be hanging around in men's shoes, but after seven aisles of women's footwear, he grabbed a pair of slippers (for her birthday; he thought) and gave up on anything masculine.

Now Sam was in the auto parts area. Really? Next to the shoes? He knew there wasn't anything on the list, but before he could move on...

"Excuse me, could I get to the motor oil?"

Was she following him? He pushed on to the household goods - pots, pans, blenders, toasters, microwaves, ovens, refrigerators, freezers, then more pots and pans. There was an egg baster. He had no idea what that was, but he knew they didn't have one. Into the cart.

A large man was walking towards him. Straight at him. In household goods.

"Don't you know my wife?"

Sam looked up at all six feet, six inches (or thereabouts) of the man. At the cut-off sleeves on the motorcycle jacket to make room for the muscles, at the tattoos of barbed wire and "Make War, Not Lov", and at the full beard circling the mouth with at least two teeth missing.

"Not, not that I know of..."

"Sure you do. From work. We met at the picnic last summer for her law firm."

"I, I don't work for a law firm. What's your wife's name?"

"Carol Warner. She's an associate. I thought you were one too."

Sam didn't know the name, but deep, deep in his mind he was almost consciously considering saying, "Oh, you mean Sugarlips?". Then the guy cracked his knuckles, and that thought died a quick death.

"No, I work in the schools. I'm a teacher." Inwardly he grimaced and thought, *I should have said I was a cop.*

The man then smiled, but it wasn't a big improvement.

"Oh, I thought you were one of those guys who is always flirting with her. You look just like him. But, nah, he had more muscle than you do, and with his hair slicked back, and no moustache."

He stuck out his hand. Sam gingerly took it and they shook, the other man's grip just strong enough to let Sam know where he stood.

"Well, have a good day anyway." The man grabbed a potholder from a pile and a bottle of dishwashing detergent and walked away. Sam took a potholder, too. You can't have too many potholders.

At the far end of the aisle, an attractive blonde flashed by. Sam at least had a direction to go now. So long as she wasn't "Carol Warner". By the time he reached that intersection, she was nowhere in sight, but he was moving.

Toys and games. Mostly for little kids. Junior (not really, his name was Bert) was eight, almost too big for many of these, so Sam looked more closely to see if there was anything more appropriate.

"May I help you, sir?"

Sam looked up and saw Gerald leaning against a display, breathing heavily. *How did he get here? This was a long way from the front door for him to go.*

"Didn't I see you at the front door?"

In a trembling voice, "Yes, sir, but that shift has ended. I am now in children's toys. Is there, hah, anything that I can help you with?"

"Uh, no .... I'm, uh, just looking for my, uh, son."

"Oh, is he missing?"

"No, I meant for something for him. He's about, uh ..." Sam raised his hand halfway up his body. It wasn't probably anywhere near Bert's actual height, but whatever.

"Whatever you say, sir. If you need any assistance, I will be right here, or right there, if I can find a chair."

Gerald slowly, slowly, moved away. Slowly.

"Ma'am, can I help you?"

Sam looked further in that direction and saw the large woman with the umpteen kids. "Mommy, can we get...? Mommy, I want... Mommy, I got to go..." He picked out a bag of toy soldiers, actually cowboys and Native-Americans. He then pushed his cart to the adult games.

Yes, the very adult games and toys. *Who would have thought there would be a selection here.*

"Excuse me, can I get some...?"

He didn't wait to hear the rest of it and moved to the family games, where he pulled down some game involving dice and a board and few directions.

Women's clothing. Damn, he hoped Junie hadn't wanted anything there. The blonde zipped by, but he left her to it, and took twenty minutes to get through the two-thirds of the store that women's garments took up. At least Sam was now through most of it.

One rack of men's shorts, and that was it for the men's section. Then children's clothing. Junie always picked out Bert's stuff and would have appended a "but" to anything he bought for Bert. "It looks nice, but.... It's a good color, but..."

Now he was in appliances and electronics. He could spend some time in here – see just how big the new TV screens were, if there were any new video games, check out the gadgets world. Sam racked his brain, trying to think of something relevant that would give him a good excuse to look around. A GPS? No, they used their phones now for that. Did Junie need something for her camera? He was sure she would have emphasized that. How about the DVDs? They had a good collection of old TV series, but that was more him than her. But, just in case, he browsed for a little while, making a mental note of possible birthday gifts for himself, or Bert. Oh, what the heck. He picked up the first season of *Washington Slept Here*, a popular family sitcom about the mayor of a small Midwestern town, for both of them.

Sam couldn't think of any more ways to waste time in this section. Except for the new refrigerators with drink dispensers for more than just water. Apparently, you can now hook it up for beer (just keep it away from the kids). And some of them even had a television screen implanted in the middle. Now you didn't have to go get a beer only during commercials. If there was somewhere to relieve yourself, you could just sit in front of your fridge all day long and never get up.

Time to move on to the groceries. This probably comprised most of Junie's list. He knew there were some food items that you could get only at the Jumbomart Supermegastore. If he only remembered what they were.

In the dairy section, Gerald was trying to add more gallon milk jugs to the milk display, but he was having a hard time lifting and placing. Sam hadn't realized he had spent enough time in the videos for Gerald to move so far.

"Here, let me help you with that." Sam took the jug from him and put it into place.

"Thank you, sir, but this is what I get paid to do."

"Okay." Sam took the next jug quickly from him and set it on his buggy. That was one less Gerald was going to have to handle.

"Excuse me, can I get to the butter?" The elderly lady again.

Gerald quickly straightened and stepped spryly to that section.

"Certainly, Madam. Let me get that for you. One pound or two?"

"Oh, let's go with two. The spreadable kind. You never know when it may come in handy."

Sam had been going to get some butter too, but decided to let the couple have their moment in private. He picked up a dozen eggs, and ignored the cottage cheese and yogurt. If they were on the list, they could stay there.

He saw the blonde turn the corner out of paper goods. Toilet paper went into the cart. Whether it was on the list or not, you couldn't go wrong with toilet paper. Maybe a roll of aluminum foil while he was at it.

A loaf of bread, a jug of wine, and thou. Add a little cheese, and he could tell Junie that thoughts of a romantic picnic had distracted him. Though Bert would also have to go on the picnic. Which meant chips and hot dogs and no further thoughts of romance.

The aisle of cleaning supplies. He had no idea which detergent to get, laundry or dishes, so grabbed both.

"Mommy, I want..." Not detergent. Maybe the next aisle was cookies. But it was soups and international foods. *Really? Those kids wanted something from India or Mexico?* Well, Sam wanted taco mixes and also Weetabix from Great Britain. The Great Britain selection was small – not very many distinctive foods from there. Ah, a sixpack of Orangina, you couldn't get that in their neighborhood store.

Cereals, crackers, and coffees. The three Cs. A box from each of some little-known brand, to justify having gone this far to buy them. He didn't even know they had coffee in a box.

He skipped the canned fruits and vegetables. Produce would hold better choices.

In the next aisle, he found Gerald helping his new friend with an extra-large jar of very creamy peanut butter and moved past. It was amazing how fast Gerald was moving now.

And Sam was moving quickly, too. He had been shopping long enough. Two packs of cookies – Bert's favorite and something new, and the extra-dark chocolate candy bar that he knew Junie loved.

Juices and soft drinks. He looked for that ginger ale that was associated with one of those young adult movies that were popular now, and was mildly surprised when he actually found it.

At the end of the aisle were the meats, and the last of the blonde leaving again. He found bratwurst, and chorizo, and mettwurst, and Italian sausage, and kielbasa, and breakfast sausage patties and links. For some reason, Junie never bought any of these, so Sam stocked up. For her, one filet of steel-head trout should do it.

The frozen foods were next. Tempting, tempting, tempting. Instant dinners, ice creams, pizzas. Ok, a pizza with everything. For supper tonight, in case he was supposed to have gotten something else. In the likelihood that he was supposed to have gotten something else.

Finally, produce, and beyond the produce, were the checkout lines. The end was in sight. He scanned quickly, looking for stuff he couldn't normally get. Uglifruit went in the buggy, plantains, pluots, Newfoundland cabbage,

French onions, ("Excuse me, can I get to the garlic paste?"), white asparagus from Germany, Peruvian lima beans. Whatever looked different.

Gerald appeared. "Let me take your cart for you, sir."

Sam was surprised enough to let him, and found that Gerald was good enough to find a checkout lane that was empty and far away from the "Mommy, we want..." family.

After unloading everything, he thought to check his pockets for the checkbook. Amazingly, he had remembered that.

Sam looked at his watch as he headed toward the car. Two and a half hours. More shopping time than he would have wished on anyone, though he knew Junie would just have been getting started. As he had personally experienced.

He loaded everything in the trunk, then opened the driver's door... and stopped dead in his tracks.

On the front seat was a piece of paper that looked suspiciously like a list. A shopping list. The shopping list. He picked it up, glancing briefly, just long enough to realize it actually was very short, but not long enough to read what he should have gotten. He didn't want to know.

Looking around the parking lot, he balled up the paper in his fist, but didn't see a nearby trashcan. However, two cars away, a back window was open about two inches. He walked over to the car, didn't see anyone close by, and pushed the paper through the cracked window, quickly jumping back as a yapping dog suddenly appeared at the window. Now he knew why it was slightly cracked.

Sam went back to the car, got in, and drove away, hoping that the note might be eaten, finally destroying all evidence.

If... your grandfather once told you a story about an experience that shook him to the bones, and left him frightened of shadows for the rest of his life, would you try to track down where that event happened, hoping to understand his fear? Or would you rather not know any more about it ...?

THE RISE OF
THE HOUSE OF USHER

The morning dawned grey, as much as it could be considered dawning. Not the grey of a morning portending a day of rain, but the grey deep in the melancholy of a man's soul, the grey that has never seen a shade of color, the grey that reminds one of the sorrows and disappointments of a lifetime.

The despair of the sky had been with me since the previous evening when I had first arrived in this colorless, godforsaken land. My journey had brought me, at last, within a few hours' ride of where I hoped to find the remains of the infamous house of Roderick Usher, the residence wherein he and his sister, Madeline, had supposedly perished as the building came down around them.

My grandfather, the sole survivor and narrator of the original story had, prior to his death, regaled me with tales of his narrow escape, but had left few clues as to its location, warning that it was an evil place better left undisturbed for all eternity. However, I could not have been my father's son, nor my grandfather's grandson, had I not made some effort to rediscover the origin of so many of my grandparent's nightmares.

It had been with the assistance of certain documents and letters found among my grandfather's estate that I had been led to the general area, and the further aid of local merchants, who had informed me that a specific area deep in the woods had long been spoken of only in whispers behind locked doors, that then brought me to what I believed to be the end of my quest. The local story was that a great tragedy of death and horror, of horror and death, had occurred within that unholy forest, and that anyone who had attempted to enter within the last fifty years had not returned to speak of it. The first only confirmed my grandfather's despondency and terror, but the second strengthened my resolve to rend the invisible curtain of the unknown, and determine once and for all time the fate of the House of Usher.

As a road to that section of the forbidding woods no longer existed, I left my carriage in the care of the innkeeper, and alone rode horseback along a little-used trail. The morning grew even greyer, though I would not have thought that possible, and the trail became dimmer and more difficult to discern. However, that did seem to be an indication that I was progressing in the correct direction, and so I continued. It was the increasing cold that seeped through my heavy overcoat that disturbed me more, as I had not planned for such a drastic change in the temperature as I ventured further among the trees and overgrown brush.

I reached a point where the horse would not continue until I had dismounted and led it, somewhat forcibly, along a path of my own making.

Though I was now well within the boundaries of the forbidden area, I had seen nothing to signify the terror with which the locals had viewed this spot. But I had also not found signs to indicate this as the site of the Usher mansion. And, had begun, for the first time, to question if I would.

My horse stopped.

And no amount of gentle, or even forceful prodding, could induce it to go further. It was a certain knowledge that, without the horse, I would stand little chance of returning to civilization. The grey had not lifted; the cold had not dissipated, and I slowly became aware that there was no movement or sound, no birds or forest creatures.

With initial stirrings of uneasiness, I spoke out loud, "I am William Little, and I have no fear of this place." The horse was momentarily startled, but nothing else stirred. The loneliness of my words, rather than fortifying my courage, quietly lingered and left me feeling even more isolated than before.

I reluctantly tethered the horse to a tree, where the animal nervously stood. Gradually, I realized that there was something significant, something unique about the very ground upon which I now tread. I searched for a place to sit, so that I could consider what was to be done. I espied a small raised clump and began to clear it off. It appeared at first to be rock, but, as I continued to clear it, I soon realized it was stone, but formed stone.

With trembling fingers, I quickly tore the grass and sod from it, discovering several stones placed together to form the foundation of a wall, a stone wall.

I followed the line of the wall to my left and began to discern the vague outline of a building. It had been lost amidst the brush and encroachment of the forest, but now that I knew what to look for, was becoming visible to my eye.

The horse had stopped just outside the wall. Its animal sense had granted it a knowledge that my human vision had not. I now stood within the confines of the wall and followed the perimeter.

As I walked, I began to recognize the overall shape of the house and occasionally stepped away from the wall to explore the ground itself. I came upon a plate and then a piece of glass, and then what appeared to be the arm from a chair.

Lost in the euphoria over the discoveries, I no longer felt the cold of the weather, but I did experience a chill rivaling that from the tales told by my grandfather, and the proof of those macabre stories was now held in my hands.

I dropped the objects and continued, but yet more warily and more spiritually deflated.

I came upon the great fireplace. It had originally been more strongly reinforced than its neighboring walls and now stood supported by a small tree. I turned, realizing this must have been the room in which my grandfather had last seen Roderick Usher. My imagination took root, visualizing the two of them sitting before the fire, Roderick's growing apprehension, the great door bursting open, and the vision of his sister, his presumed deceased sister, the sister whose illness had brought him such agony, standing there before him.

I blinked, and the scene disappeared. But not at once, only gradually fading away, as if it was stubbornly resisting leaving.

The horse reared, as if it too had experienced something it did not understand.

As I stepped toward it, my boot struck something solid. I kicked at it, but it refused to move. Kneeling, I brushed the dirt away, and realized it was the top of a long great table that must have stood in the room. I wondered what other objects might be buried here, then jumped as my hands brushed against something round and hard. Reluctantly, and with the beginnings of dread, I reached back down and carefully cleared away enough dirt to bring the object upward.

It was a skull. A human skull.

I nearly dropped it, but recovered in time. There was, of course, no way to identify it as either Roderick or Madeline. It may even have been a servant, but my grandfather's recountings of the incident did not refer to any domestic being present in the room.

I wiped it clean of dirt, then set it gingerly upon the remains of the table, facing away from me. As a rule, I am not superstitious, but the day and the dismal atmosphere had induced in me an underlying depression that I was finding it difficult to discount.

I backed away from that room as I was anxious lest I find something else equally disturbing.

Following the outline, I came upon a large bush. Upon closer inspection, I saw it covered a portion of interior wall. I followed it to a corner, then around the corner to an even larger section of wall, less hidden and more clearly not part of nature. I stepped away from the wall and looked back toward the horse. I could dimly perceive it at the far end of the outline of the house, an outline that appeared to be much more distinct than I had originally perceived. How could I not have recognized it in the first place? It was so obvious now, with the walls and foundation exceedingly apparent. I could even begin to make out what seemed to be mounds of furniture. The weeds and ground growth also appeared to have receded.

I turned back to the wall in front of me and was surprised at how long and high it now appeared. From where the horse pawed at the ground, it struck me as nearly impossible for me not to have seen this structure at once. A door frame still stood in the middle of the wall and I passed through.

There were three almost complete walls standing, a nearly complete room. This was extraordinary that this could have withstood the ravages of the elements for fifty years. Unbelievably extraordinary, in fact. The cold within me intensified.

Passing through another doorway in the far wall, I now came upon a complete room, missing only a ceiling. A table even stood against a wall. And above it was an intact window. That could not be! I rubbed my eyes, but the scene persisted. I strode to the window and looked out, at a green lawn and a garden! In shock, I backed into the table. It was sturdier than I had reason to expect and, looking down on it, it now appeared new and imposing, not the weather-beaten table I had first assumed.

With a cry, I turned and ran back through the doorway. But it was not the three-walled room I now entered, but another full room with a ceiling. I no longer knew which way I was running, but continued through doorway after doorway, each one bringing me to a room now looking newer and filled with more furniture.

"No!" I shouted and heard an answering whinny from a great distance away. "Where are you?" My voice shook with the fear that I had been trying with great difficulty not to acknowledge.

I chose a door in the direction where I believed I had heard the horse. There were no longer any windows to see outside the house and I could not find a door exiting to the outside world.

The horror was beginning to overwhelm me, the realization that the house was rebuilding itself around me. The House of Usher. The house that knew only fear and sorrow. The house that had destroyed itself rather than continue to experience the emotional intensity of its occupant.

Out of breath, I paused for a moment. Then I heard a sound. Not the horse, but... No, it couldn't be...

Voices carried on the wind. Indistinct, barely a murmur at first, but growing. There, coming from there. I moved into the next room, but stopped as a fresh fear grew in me. I now heard two voices, a man and a woman. I still could not distinguish what they were saying, but I knew, oh, yes, I knew, that there was no one else here but me.

I remembered the skull I had found. I whirled around the room I was in and noted the restoration of the furniture, the portraits on the wall, and even the lit lamp. What else could come back? What else? What unspeakably terrifying image?

I could not go on. My horse may have been in that direction, but also the great room, the room with the voices, the room with the unknown, but, even more, the horror, the unknowable!

I fled in the other direction. I do not know how many rooms I passed through or for how long I ran, but I did know it was away from the voices. Until...

I heard them again.

There is no escape. No matter where I go, I hear the voices. Time has no meaning. Daylight may have come and gone, and come again. I have no way of knowing.

For my grandfather, horror had its limitations. Mine has none. I have heard the first distinct word spoken by the voices.

"Madeline."

If... you were about to be hung for a crime that you did commit, would you grab on to any scrap of hope for a rescue, any sign that you might survive into the rest of the day?

AN INCIDENT AT THORNE FORKS

The rope hung, ever so slightly swaying in the breeze. It waved about five and a half feet above a trapdoor in the platform, which suddenly sprang open. The man operating the mechanism smiled to himself and set it back in place. He signaled over to another man standing in front of the jail, and called, "It's alright, sheriff. It's ready to go whenever you are. I mean, whenever he is." The sheriff only nodded and remained where he was.

Peterson squinted out at the scene from behind the cell bars of his window, chewing a plug of tobacco. The sun had been up only an hour, but there had been much activity around the platform in that hour. And it had all been for him. "My, my. There's more to-do over my demise than there ever was over my being born." He spat through the bars.

He could see all the comings and goings of the dusty town of Thorne Forks from this window. More and more people had been gathering since sunup and they were all waiting for him to put in a final appearance in half an hour or so.

He twisted his neck so he could see the west end of town. "Well, it looks like I'm going to be left on my own." He raised his voice. "Thanks a lot, you dirty, low-down, horse-stealing sons of bitches. I get caught and the rest of you go free, and what the hell do you care? You can just pocket my share from that cattle we rustled, now can't you?" He turned back to the cell. "Damnation."

Peterson sat down on the lone cot, careful not to just fall on it because the ancient thing was bound to collapse at any moment. He watched a many-legged insect slowly making its way across the floor toward the light from the window. "Hey, bug," he whispered. "Hey there, bug, can't you get out of here either? Won't your friends come and help you out? ... Well, my friends won't help me neither. Hah! Friends? What friends? They're gonna leave me here to die and I can't do a damn thing about it. Me! I'm the one that planned the whole blasted thing! They never could have done it without me. They're nothin' by themselves and they're gonna let me die. Do you believe that, bug? Do you believe that they could do that to me?"

The bug had stopped, almost as if it had been listening to him. But now there was no sound. Peterson realized with a start that there was no noise coming from outside either. The infernal chattering of the crowd had stopped and a strange silence had taken over.

He hurried to his window and looked outside. Every single face in the crowd was turned toward the road leading from the east. A lone rider, framed by the morning sun, was coming.

He was dressed all in black – the hat, the shirt, vest and pants, the boots, and even the spurs – all black. And he was riding the darkest horse that Peterson had ever seen. As he rode closer, they could see that he had a small black moustache whose ends curled up. The brim of his hat shaded his eyes, but Peterson could still make out two small malevolent dots of light glaring out at the townspeople.

The crowd silently parted as he passed through and rode up to the saloon. He dismounted, glared once more around the gathering, and passed inside. One man broke loose from the crowd and ran up to the sheriff still standing in front of the jail.

"Ain't you goin' to do something 'bout that, WT? Look at that face and those clothes, he has to be wanted for somethin'. Or he might be here to try and spring Peterson. You better arrest him or somethin'."

The sheriff of Thorne Forks, WT Short, turned and spat a wad of tobacco to his right, then stared for a long time over at the saloon door. He had been born with the name "Short" but he also had the unfortunate circumstance of being blessed with a similar stature. His courage was not that limited, but then neither was his knowledge of the law. He looked back at the man that had approached him.

"He ain't on any wanted posters, Henry. I ain't likely to forget a face like that. And he ain't done nothing here yet. Henry, you can't arrest a man just cause he dresses like a villain." He turned his gaze over to Peterson, still staring out of the cell window. "And I don't rightly think he's goin' to be gettin' rescued. The other members of the gang each get a bigger split without him around."

Peterson turned around and slid down the wall until he was sitting on the floor. His body was shaking with both laughter and relief. "Those fools. That guy has to be here to save me. On the day that a fierce outlaw, namely me, is going to be hanged, a mean-lookin' character just happens to come ridin' in. Sure, and I bet he ordered a glass of milk in that saloon, too."

He looked down at the insect still sitting in the pool of sunlight. "Looks like I do have friends after all, bug." He leaned in, whispering, "I'm gettin' out of here, bug, ... and when I go, you go." He sat back again and winked at the silent creature.

The noise of the crowd had risen again after the stranger had passed inside, but it began to slowly die as the hour of the execution neared. A restlessness began among the people. A hanging was a rare thing in Thorne Forks, but, after all, there were businesses that had to be gotten back to.

Sheriff Short peered up at the sun, then turned to the slight, bespectacled man next to him. "I guess it's about time." The man nodded and went over to take his place on the platform as the executioner.

Peterson heard them coming for him and looked back from his post at the window with a start. The man in black had not come out of the saloon yet. *He must be plannin' on makin' a big scene out of it*, he thought. *Rescuin' me right out from under the rope.* He leaned down to the bug and poked it

29

with his finger to make sure it was still alive. It scurried a few inches before he managed to pick it up.

He straightened up just as the sheriff reached the cell door.

"It's time, Peterson."

He nodded, trying to hide a thin smile. *But time for what, sheriff?* He was confident now. The people would merely think he was facing his death like a man. But he knew better.

When they reached the porch, he suddenly bent down and released the bug he had been holding onto the wooden planks. Short had moved forward with his hand on his gun, but frowned when he saw what Peterson had done.

Peterson smiled up at him. "Just lettin' one of your prisoners go, Sheriff. Might's well get all the residents out at one time."

He tried very hard to keep from smiling as they passed through the crowd on their way to the platform. He didn't want to disappoint them too early. They'd seen hardened criminals before, but for most of them, it was their first hanging. They'd get to see what a man looked like, just as he knew he was about to die.

They led him up the steps, tied his hands behind his back, and placed the noose over his head. A man of the cloth stepped in front of him and started reading from the Bible. But Peterson wasn't listening to the words. His eyes were roaming wildly over the crowd and for the first time, the signs of strain and worry began to show themselves on his face. The stranger hadn't shown up yet. *He sure is cuttin' it close,* Peterson thought. Then, just as the minister finished his words and headed for the steps, he saw the man in black step out of the saloon behind the crowd, take a toothpick out of his mouth and flick it to the ground. He slowly began to draw his gun out of his holster.

A wild feeling rose up in Peterson's chest and he couldn't keep the grin from his face any longer, as he silently cheered the stranger on. *Yeah, I knew you would be here. You wouldn't let me down. C'mon, shoot now, will ya? I haven't got all day. Just shoot the damn*

Satisfied that his gun was loaded, the stranger slipped it back into his holster and wiped the last of the milk from his mouth. He had been told that there was a band of ruthless outlaws in the direction he was heading, and it might be handy to be prepared for them.

He settled himself on his horse and glanced over at the body softly swaying in the breeze. *Sure is a damn fool way to die*, he thought. *With a silly grin on his face like that.* He shook his head and rode off into the west.

I'VE SEEN THE MORNING RISE

I've seen the morning rise on rainy days
In silent ways
Before the sun comes to.
I've seen the evenings set on stormy nights
Without the lights
To guide believers through.
I've watched the mothers bring their daughters home
And sit alone
And wait for storms to break.
I've watched the fathers take their only sons
When they were done
And teach them how to take.
I've watched the rivers flow through wounded fields
They could not heal
Until they'd turned to sand.
I've watched the hillsides empty of their trees
Without a breeze
To cool the brow of man.

But now

But now

Now I see the mornings rise on springtime days
In gentle ways
To bring alive our souls.
I see the evenings set on autumn nights
Let forth the lights
Remind us we are whole.
I watch the mothers bring their daughters home
To teach them on their own
And show them how to live.
I watch the father take their only sons
To watch the rivers run
And teach them how to give.
I watch the rivers run through fields of green
Bring back where they have been
And show us what to do.
I watch the hillsides growing full of trees
Remind us of a life to see
For we will make it through.
We will make it through.

If ... you were a ghost, but you were haunted more by the human that was currently living in your home, what would you do? Would you just let things go, or would you try to do something about it?

THE HAUNTING OF MR. BLOFF

George Ivan Chumley was not a happy ghost.

It is tempting to say that he was, in fact, pissed. But it is difficult to refer to ghosts as pissed, in either the drunk or urinary manner, so we'll just say this ghost was not happy.

The house that he was haunting, that he had been haunting, that it was his job to haunt, had, up to this point, been basically a happy place to work. The Thompson family that had been there for twenty years had been a genuinely joyful family. Three children, a loving mother and father, pets that had come and gone. One of the pets, the raven, Buzzy, had perished right here in the house in a rather tragic way, dive-bombing into a mirror because he had been so happy to see another raven in the house. The broken mirror, of course, meant seven years' bad luck for Buzzy, but that didn't matter much to him because he was already, well, dead. However, it did mean that he got to join Chumley in haunting the house.

For Chumley, haunting was not the scary kind. Except, naturally, for Halloween, when you were supposed to scare all the neighborhood kids. Every year, the Thompsons always wondered why they had so much leftover candy when there were obviously so many children running around in the neighborhood. They just seemed to be more running away from rather than running towards the house. But every October, it meant more candy for the

Thompson kids to eat over the next several weeks, and they were happy about that.

But Chumley did not want to scare the Thompsons away. The children – Shirley, Edith, and Frederick – actually seemed to enjoy having a ghost, or, at least, something else around. There were times when toys were mysteriously picked up, or beds were suddenly made that had nothing to do with them. If a door creaked open or a noise came from the attic, it also, usually, had nothing to do with them. Even the occasional unexpected cawing from Buzzy simply reminded them fondly of a deceased, well-loved pet.

As for their parents, any sudden noises or unexplained events probably just meant the kids were doing something they weren't supposed to, and the parents were better off not knowing about it until they had to, anyway.

But good times could not last forever. The children grew up and moved away, and the Thompsons decided they needed a smaller place in a warmer climate, near one of the kids.

That's when Mr. Bloff moved in.

At first, Chumley and Buzzy did not see any problem. He was an older gentleman who seemed somewhat quiet. He never invited anyone over for loud parties and never really did much of anything. It was pretty boring, but livable. Chumley and Buzzy just made sure to stay in other parts of the house, even if they had not much of anything to do or see.

Then they realized that the house itself was suffering. No cleaning was ever done. Dirty dishes stayed in the sink until Mr. Bloff would wipe one with a dirty dishtowel just to put another instant meal on. The wastebaskets overflowed, and some were never, I mean never, emptied. Laundry wasn't done. Filthy clothes stayed in piles on the floor, with Mr. Bloff sometimes picking something from the bottom to wear. That is, if he ever wanted to change out of the same old pajamas and ratty bathrobe that he almost always wore. He never washed sheets and towels. The ghosts never saw a dustrag or a vacuum, certainly not in use.

He farted. Constantly. From all the bad, non-nutritional food he was eating, and also probably from the lack of exercise. He spent the entire day sitting in front of his computer, or his television set, watching the worst reality shows or gory movies. Sometimes it was difficult to tell the difference because all the characters were so mean to each other and so terrifying. Even Chumley and Buzzy would flinch at some of the horror movies, because they didn't know any ghosts that acted like that.

But the worst part was that there was no longer any space in the house, only paths tracking his unchanging routes from one room to another. The only thing he did on his computer was order ... stuff. And order more ... stuff. The ghosts never found out what he did order, because the boxes were simply piled on top of other boxes, unopened and unused. Just something else to add to the detritus of the house.

The house, which once had held such joy and hope, became incredibly filthy, and rundown, and abandoned as anything but a roof over Mr. Bloff's head. Chumley finally decided that enough was horribly enough, and that, for the house's sake, he was going to have to act like a genuine ghost.

He first started simply, blowing air into Mr. Bloff's ear at random times. Bloff would shiver and look around, finding no one there. Then the air puff would come in the other ear. Bloff swatted at his ear, but then went back to watching somebody's heart get torn out on one of the reality shows. Chumley continued with this, but added the back door suddenly being blown open again and again, then bedspreads coming off the bed in the middle of the chilly night.

When those produced no real response, as they were more annoying than anything else, one day Chumley knocked one of the unopened boxes off a pile. It landed with a resounding crash and the unmistakable sound of something breaking. Mr. Bloff shook his head, but didn't move out of his chair. When Chumley pushed over another package, he finally roused himself with a loud groan, and a louder fart for good measure. He merely picked up the now rattling boxes and put them back on top of their piles, never checking the contents.

Chumley upended a third carton directly in front of him and finally got his attention.

Mr. Bloff stopped what he was doing and stared at the new mess on the floor. He had watched the box fall, but had no idea how it had happened. He went over and kicked at it, as if it were alive. Chumley kicked the pile back at him, and Bloff backed away until he ended up back at his chair. He sat down, faced the TV, and turned the volume way up.

Chumley knocked another box off, then another, each with a loud crash. Mr. Bloff flinched each time, but refused to turn around. Buzzy cawed in one ear, then the other, but Bloff only covered his ears with his hands and cowered lower in his chair. The back door opened and closed, opened and closed. Chumley and Buzzy looked at each other, in the way that only ghosts can. Buzzy flew down to the television remote, grasped it with both claws, and flew up straight in front of Mr. Bloff's face. Bloff watched the remote, one of his few connections to the outside world, fly away across the room and into the bathroom. He heard a splash and jumped up with a loud "No!"

He ran into the bathroom and slammed the door shut, locking it behind him. The locked door did not stop the two spirits from phasing through it and following him. After fishing the remote out of the toilet, Mr. Bloff was at the sink, running water over it, the first thing they had ever seen him try to clean. He glanced up in the mirror and saw two ghostly apparitions reflected at him over his shoulder. He whirled around, but there was nothing there. Back to the mirror, where both the man and the bird were now smiling at him. Back around, and nothing at all.

Mr. Bloff dropped the remote into the sink, where it broke apart, and ran into the door, forgetting that he had shut it. He turned the knob, but it wouldn't open, also forgetting that he had locked it. Finally getting it open, he dashed into his bedroom, got down on the floor, and pulled an old, battered suitcase out from under the bed. Grabbing an armful of dirty clothes from the pile at the foot of his bed, he stuffed as much of it into the suitcase as he could fit.

He made his way through his paths to his front door, constantly swiveling his head, as if looking for something he didn't want to see. He opened the door, then stood there for a moment. With the unfamiliar sunshine initially blinding him, he started to bring his hand up to shade his eyes, but it never got further than his chest. He suddenly clutched the chest and groaned deeply, expelling all of the air that his lungs could have held, then collapsed on the front step.

It was actually two days before any of the neighbors noticed the body lying in front of the house. By then, of course, it was too late for Mr. Bloff. Though Chumley and Buzzy had wanted him to leave, they hadn't wanted him to exit quite that way.

Within two weeks, whatever distant family there was had come and gone, and all the ... stuff had been removed. It was going to take a while before the house was clean and back to its former self, but steps were being taken.

Both Chumley and Buzzy were smiling and singing as they wandered through what they considered their house again. Maybe they would get a nice family this time. But whoever moved in couldn't be as bad as Mr. Bloff had been. He had to have been the limit.

They paused in front of a hallway mirror, which had finally been wiped down enough to show a reflection. They enjoyed seeing just the two of them for a moment. But then, slowly, another figure gradually appeared behind them, dressed in a ratty old bathrobe, and scratching under his armpit. The figure farted, loudly, then grinned.

"Good to see you again, guys."

Chumley sighed. "Oh, crap."

If... you had a photograph from an earlier time in your life that depicted the people that were important to you at that time, but then the figures started disappearing. Disappearing, not only from the picture, but from life, and from everybody's memories but your own, would you be concerned that your turn may come? That no one may remember you?

THE PHOTOGRAPH

The rain had let up considerably by the time his car pulled into the driveway, but he was still dripping when I opened the door. He strode past me without a word and headed straight into my study off the hallway, as if this was his home and not mine. I followed him in and closed the door behind me. He was standing in front of my desk, disregarding the pool of water forming on the carpet around his feet. I took his coat, shook off the excess water into the wastebasket before hanging it on the coat stand, and motioned him to the easy chair to the right of the desk, the chair reserved for my clients. I then went behind the desk to my own plush seat, waiting for him to finally give me a hint as to what he wanted.

He had called two days previously and had demanded an immediate appointment. I told him the soonest I could get him in and he had instantly agreed. He sat here now in front of me, clutching a manila envelope in his left hand, his mouth working, his teeth clenching.

I checked the appointment pad in front of me. "Mr. ... Paul Norman?" He nodded, but remained silent. "You couldn't tell me over the phone why you wanted to see me so urgently. You insisted you had to do it in person. Well, I'm waiting. Why do you need an investigator of unexplained events, and why me in particular?"

He took a deep breath, leaned forward, and sat the envelope on my desk. "Those are why I need an investigator. As for why you? Because they tell me you're the best. Everybody has heard of Allen Leighton, the man that can spot a phony out-of-this-world experience a mile away." He waved at the envelope. "I need you to find out if the photographs in there tell a real story or if somebody is trying to drive me crazy." He said it simply, but he meant it.

I pulled the envelope toward me. There was nothing on the outside but his name in the upper right-hand corner. Glancing at him, I opened it and gently pulled out two photographs. One was of a group of about eight young people gathered around a table eating dinner in what appeared to be a university cafeteria on a college campus. The other picture was of the same table, but with only three people present. The touch of professionalism was lacking, but, for an amateur, they were adequate.

I looked back at him. "Nice pictures, but the point?"

He looked at me through suddenly tired eyes. "Have you ever heard of Dorian Gray, Mr. Leighton?"

"Sure. Wasn't he the character in one of Oscar Wilde's stories whose photograph aged instead of him? He stayed young, but the picture became old and ugly as it took on all of his sins."

"It was a painting, Mr. Leighton, not a photograph. This doesn't have to do with hidden aging, but look again at those photographs. Look closely, very closely."

It was then that I noticed Norman was in both pictures. A younger Norman, maybe by a couple of years, but it was him nevertheless. And it was the exact same pose in both of them. He was seated, holding a glass in his right hand in both, turned toward his left, smiling at an empty chair in the less-populated picture, but at a young, very attractive woman in the other. Then I noticed that the other two young men in the second picture with Norman were also in the first in the same positions. Exactly. One of them, sitting just to Norman's right, was lifting a forkful of something to his mouth, and, by the look on his face, had been caught by surprise by the camera. The other one was just setting a tray laden with food down at the far end of the table.

I again looked back up at Norman. "They're the same pictures. Just with some of the people erased. Somebody did a pretty good touch-up job to get that effect. Why?"

"Nobody did any touch-up jobs. All the people missing in the second picture are dead. And not only dead, but gone. Completely gone." His tone was flat, as if there was no spirit left in his voice. "No trace of them left behind, no memory, nothing. It's as if they never existed at all."

I sat up a little straighter in my chair. This wasn't the typical "I hear my dead aunt's voice" story. "I think you better explain everything to me, Norman. Slowly, and from the beginning."

He nodded and took a deep breath, to put some life back into his lungs. "Alright, from the beginning.

"That dinner you see there in the picture was one of the last times the eight of us ate together our senior year at Bradford State. We had all been good friends and someone got the great idea to have a picture of us all together before we graduated and went our final ways. An official photograph from a real camera, not a cell phone. I was to be in charge of getting the prints developed and then getting copies out to everybody. I'll start at the far end of the table and go clockwise, giving you all their names.

"Joe Wayne was the one just setting his tray down at that far end. There were several pictures taken at the meal, but this was the only one with him in it. His roommate, Joel Sullivan, on the right side of the table, to Joe's left, was looking up at the camera. Next to him was Becky Peters, then came Beverly McCrea. The empty seat next to her belonged to Darryl Bressler, Junior – his dad owned the internationally known Bressler Electronics." I had heard of Senior, but nothing about a Junior at any time. "He's the one who had the really nice camera, so he took the pictures. The only reason he was eating with us that night was because he was dating Bev then. None of the rest of us really knew him that well. Across from where he had been sitting, ignoring the whole thing, intent on his mashed potatoes, was Lloyd Peters, Becky's brother. Between Lloyd and who I assume you recognized as me, was my roommate, Gordon Wright. He didn't realize Bressler was going to take a picture right then. Then me, and, finally, Jean Weisleman, who later became my wife."

It was his turn to look up at me. "Everybody there, except for Bressler, was immensely interested in the story of Dorian Gray. Primarily in the idea that a painting could physically take on the moral character of the subject. That any personal object could, in some way, reflect the character, the morality, the personality of its owner. Each of us wanted a copy of the photograph, so that we could observe it down through the years and maybe find out what kind of degenerates the rest of us had become. It was more out of fun and curiosity that we wanted to do it, rather than any true scientific expectations.

"That first picture shows just how it was that night. A week and a half later, on a Friday night, I had received the prints and had already sealed all the individual envelopes when I heard over the radio that there had been a terrible bus accident and fourteen people had been killed. Both Lloyd and Becky Peters, Bev McCrea, and Darryl Bressler were all on that bus going home for the weekend. Nothing was ever heard about them after that night. We saw nothing about them in the papers, but some bodies were burned beyond recognition and we knew that was their bus, so we assumed they were among the unrecognizable. Calling their cell phones reached nothing. We knew they were gone. We never heard anything about funerals, so never went. None of the rest of us knew their families, so it wasn't until a few years later, when I investigated it on my own, that I discovered there should have been eighteen bodies. For that's how many got on that bus that didn't get off. But the fourteen bodies, including the difficult to identify, that were found didn't include my friends." He shifted in his seat and dropped his eyes. "And that's not the worst of it. When I discovered their bodies were unaccounted for, I tried to contact their families and old friends. But nobody had ever heard of them. It was as if God had looked back on their lives, decided they were mistakes, and simply erased them to start over.

"They were no longer in my copy of the photograph, either. I insisted they had been there, but the others, who had not seen the picture before the accident, were convinced that I must have been mistaken. Only the five of us remembered them, though we didn't know it at the time.

"That was the first incident. The second one occurred within a year after that. Joel Sullivan disappeared overseas as a member of the armed forces in a combat area. And he disappeared from the picture, too. Not at once, but about two weeks after he was reported missing. This time, there was no doubt he had originally been in it. The first time I never thought to check the prints belonging to the missing people. Oddly, it turned out theirs haven't changed at all. But this time, both Jean and Gordon agreed that something was happening. It appeared to be what we called, for lack of anything better, the 'Dorian Gray Syndrome'. An unexplained phenomenon, and sad because it was happening to our friends, but we never really considered the personal consequences."

He rubbed his forehead with his right hand. "I have no idea if Joe Wayne realized what was happening. I haven't seen or heard from him since the day we graduated."

Norman stood up and walked over to the window. "I didn't really think about what it would mean to be forgotten, to be as if you had never existed, until a couple of months ago. My wife died then, quite suddenly. And then she disappeared from the picture." He turned back to me. "Her parents had never heard of her before. Her sister had never heard of her. She had never existed for them." He shook his head, his eyes glistening with tears in remembrance. "What finally made me decide I had to do something about it was when a close friend of mine came up to me last week and asked me when I was thinking of leaving the life of the carefree bachelor and settling down." He took a deep, shuddering breath. "I decided I had to come to you. Am I going mad? Is it really happening or is somebody trying to drive me crazy? I want you to investigate this and find out."

I swiveled my chair around to face him better, doodling on my notepad to keep my hands occupied. His story had been fascinating, and he almost had me believing it. But, of course, it was just another attempt to put one over on the expert. Either that or somebody was doing a good job of driving him around the proverbial bend. But it couldn't be true. It definitely couldn't be true.

However, I was willing to take his money. "Give me the names and addresses of everybody connected with this. I'll see what I can do. I can promise you that if anything is fraudulent here, I'll know it. And you'll be the first one I tell."

He smiled then for the first time and walked back over to the desk, pulling a piece of paper out of his pocket and placing it on top of the pictures. "This includes the last address I had for Joe Wayne. Thank you, thank you very much. You've eased an enormous burden from my mind. I can't tell you how much it's going to mean to me, whatever you find. But find something. I don't want to be forgotten."

I walked him to the door and shook hands with him. The sun was shining brightly by now and the puddles on the street had started to already dry up. I went back to the office to have a closer look at those pictures, and glanced up at the window just as he was pulling out of the driveway. Then it happened.

A car came careening around the corner straight for him, clearly going too fast and clearly not in control enough to avoid him. Norman had no chance. It smashed into the driver's side, completely crushing him.

Instinctively, I hurried to the hall, thinking that maybe, against all odds, there was still something I could do to help. I threw open the door and stopped.

There was nothing. No accident, no bloody mess, only a car traveling too quickly down the far end of the street. I walked slowly out to the road, not understanding what had happened. I bent down and looked closely at the pavement. There were no skid marks. I looked back at the window from which I had watched, and the thought hit me. Jumping up, I sprinted inside, faster than I had run in years.

The photographs were lying undisturbed on my desk. But the second one was the one I needed to see. Wayne was still just setting his tray down, and Wright was still surprised. But all around them were empty seats.

Paul Norman did not exist anymore. And, according to the photograph, Paul Norman had never existed.

The list of names and addresses that he had given me was still there. I picked it up and studied it. It contained the names of all the people present at that last dinner, as well as the families of everyone except Wayne. There were question marks under his address and family. Gordon Wright's address was given as a hospital in Houston. No mention was made of what was wrong with him, but he was my best remaining chance of finding out what was going on. I had to talk to him.

His mother, living in Baltimore, was the only family he had left. He had never married and, outside of his friends at the last dinner, had apparently never become close to anyone else.

I gave the mother a call. No one was going to be paying my fee or even expenses. But I was stuck in it now. There was no turning back.

As I had feared, she could not recall any Paul Norman and insisted that her son had a room to himself during his senior year in school. None of the other names, not even Wayne's, made any impression on her. When I asked about her son being in a hospital, she became very quiet for a few minutes. Once she came back, in a choked voice, she told me he had been there for quite a while. He had cancer and probably didn't have long to live. I said I was very sorry, thanked her for her help, and hung up, cursing to myself.

That didn't give me much time. I was going to have to hurry if I hoped to get anything out of Wright. Not only were the people in that photograph completely disappearing in death, they were disappearing from life at a very fast rate.

Two days later, I was in Houston's St. Theresa Hospital. At first, they refused to let me see Wright because he was under constant intensive care and I was not a member of the family. But enough people owed me favors, even down in Houston, for some strings to be pulled and I was escorted in to see him in the late afternoon.

He was very pale and very weak. He seemed happy that someone had come all the way from Ann Arbor, Michigan, just to talk to him, but it was agony for him to move at all and he had difficulty just shaking hands. His disease was in a very advanced state. Because the doctors had told me it was hard for him to talk, and I could not ask him to repeat anything, I had brought a tape recorder and held it up for him.

We talked for over half an hour, taking it slow, but the only thing he could add about it all was that Joe Wayne had planned on becoming an electrical engineer after college. The doctors shooed me out at the end of the half hour, saying Wright needed his rest.

For the next four days, I tried to get back in to see him, but each time I was told he was too exhausted, the memories and the effort to talk had taken their toll on him. On the fifth day, he died.

I assume he died. The hospital staff denied ever having a patient under that name, and certainly not as recently as the day before. I called Mrs. Wright, who said she thought Gordon was a fine name for a boy. She wished she had a son to give that name to, but she never had. She was sorry, but her only child had been a daughter who had died at the age of six. I replayed the conversation with Wright on the tape recorder. All I heard were questions being asked with no answering responses. Back in my hotel room, the second photograph showed a young man setting down a tray of food at the head of a long, empty table.

Gordon Wright did not exist anymore. Only two people now knew that Wright had ever existed at all.

It's been three years since Wright died. I have spent most of that time in looking for Joe Wayne. He was the sole survivor, and there had to be an answer. I almost reached him three months ago. Only an hour out of Seattle, where he was reported working, the radio informed me of another disaster. The building in which he worked had burned down. It was later proven to have been arson. The company had financial problems and needed the insurance money. No bodies were ever found in the ashes and wreckage, and no employees were reported missing, so murder was not included in the charges, but I knew it should have been. Joe Wayne had disappeared from the photograph.

I returned home to Ann Arbor, but there was really nothing to come back to. In my wild search for Wayne, I had let my practice go. I had some money left, but with the end of the photograph's victims, there was nothing left to spur me on. I had no heart for anything else.

In the last three months, my health has deteriorated. My doctor tells me that if I don't pull out of this depression soon, I'm just going to waste away into nothingness. He can't understand it, but I can and that is why I am writing this, hoping something will remain of this whole affair.

For almost three years, I had been under the impression that I was the only one, not actually in the picture, who had been involved in what had followed, so I never perceived it as potentially impacting me personally. But soon after Wayne died, I realized I was wrong. I was not the only one. There had been the photographer, Darryl Bressler. And what had happened to him? He had disappeared along with the rest. Am I going to go the same way? Just because I know about it? Oh, God, what is going to happen to me? Oh, God ...

The door creaked and blew up a small cloud of dust as it swung back on its hinges. The real estate agent coughed and flailed at the air, driving the dust further back into the house. He stepped aside and gestured for the young couple to precede him.

"I told you it hasn't been occupied in years. Doesn't look as if it's even seen the light of day in all that time." He looked pleadingly at the young bride. "Sure you want to see this place, Mrs. Warren? Even if I say so myself, it's not the best place in Ann Arbor."

She gripped her husband's arm firmly and led him off the hall into what must have once been a study. "Yes, Mr. Lester, this is just the kind of place we're looking for. Right, Gary?"

Her husband meekly smiled back at Lester and shrugged his shoulders. "Anything you say, honey."

She continued around the room. "Look, we could put a bookcase in that corner, and – what's this?" She bent to pick up a photograph lying on the floor. "Why, that's a peculiar subject to take a picture of. And look, there's no dust on it. It must have just gotten here not too long ago."

"Let me take a look at that." Lester reached out his hand. "Hmm, that is pretty odd. Somebody else looking at the place must have left this behind. I'll have to check around and see if anything else has been disturbed."

He reached into his pocket and drew out a packet of matches. "But I might as well get rid of this now for you." As it started to flame up, he set it into the fireplace. "Not much to it. Just a long empty table with several food trays around it. And that's all." He turned back to the Warrens. "Well, we better go look at the rest of the house while there's still light."

He turned back at the door just as the flame went out in the fireplace and all that remained were ashes.

"That's funny. I thought I heard somebody moan." He shrugged his shoulders and left, shutting the door behind him.

THE POWER OF WINTER

Snowy plains
And whitened treefall
Remind us all
Of nature's wrath.

Frightened hare
And lonely owl call
Lead us down
The unfamiliar path.

I can hear
The way the wind blows
Whistling through
The naked trees.

I can feel
The cold in my bones
As I worship here
On bended knee.

I can see
Unbroken snowfall
Across the fields
And to the hills.

No one walks
In morning silence
As nature's power
Fulfills its will.

If ... you were in the middle of writing a story, and you suddenly received a phone call from one of your characters, a character who doesn't exist outside of your imagination, how would you react? Would you be excited, ... or just the slightest bit anxious?

THE CALLER

The cellphone chimed.

Ian Marshall looked up from the laptop and the story he was currently writing, and frowned at the noisy interruption. He let it go to voicemail, but the caller didn't leave a message. He tried to resume his train of thought, but the phone rang again. Again, he let it go. Again, no message.

The third time, he reached over in annoyance and picked it up.

"Hello!" His voice was louder than he usually used, but, after all, this was his work time.

"Hello, is this Andrew?"

He sighed. A wrong number. He took another breath and spoke in a calmer voice. "I'm sorry, you must have the wrong number. There is no Andrew here."

"Thank you. I am sorry." Click.

He shook his head and tried to go back to work. But it was no good. His concentration was shot, and he glanced up at the wall clock. It was close to four-thirty and his dinner routine was five o'clock at the diner across the street. He closed the laptop and shuffled through former story drafts until it was time.

George Glass, the proprietor, set the already-prepared cup of coffee down on the counter as soon as he walked in the door.

"Good to see you again this evening, Mr. Marshall, sir." Glass' eyes twinkled as he greeted him.

"George, how many times do I have to tell you to stop calling me, 'Mr. Marshall'? The 'sir' is enough," Marshall replied in exasperation, but with a smile. "I swear, I'm going to start doing my own cooking, and then my death from malnutrition will be on your conscience. Though, with the kind of food you serve, my death will probably be on your conscience, anyway."

"Yes, sir, anything you say, sir." Glass couldn't resist emphasizing the 'sir'.

Marshall frowned at him, then picked up his menu and glanced down the too-familiar list. "I think I'll have something different tonight. Something to get me in the mood for finishing my novel. Do you happen to have any beef jerky?"

Glass laughed. "So, you're still working on that Western story." He added a glass of water, no ice, two lemon slices, to the counter. "How many more Andrews, Osbournes, and Smiths have those two brothers killed?" He chuckled. "I still don't know where you came up with the idea of two brothers killing everybody else who had the same name. And their last name had to be Smith yet."

"How many people do you think would get killed if their last name was Leibowitz or Hammerschmidt or something? Huh?" They both laughed at that. "Anyway, they've only got one last Andrew Smith to kill ... and I haven't decided yet if I'm going to have him be a distant cousin or not. He might even survive the book and the brothers might not. I just don't know yet." He looked again at the menu. "But I'm still hungry, so give me some of that ... chop suey. Maybe I'll make him Chinese."

When he had finished his dinner, Marshall returned home and, as he usually did, studied the Philadelphia Phillies box score in depth.

The cellphone chimed.

Marshall looked at the phone in surprise and then at his watch. *Now, who can that be*, he thought. *Duane isn't supposed to call for another hour. Maybe something unexpected came up.*

"Hello."

"Hello, is Andrew there?"

He looked up at the ceiling. Not again. "I'm sorry, you must have the wrong number. There is no Andrew here."

"Thank you, I apologize." Click.

I wonder who Andrew is, he thought. *He's not getting his phone calls.* He looked once again at the phone, and, as he frequently did when in his writer's mood, spoke out loud. "If that guy ever calls again, I think I'll say 'Yes, I'm Andrew.' If he starts to get into anything personal, I'll just say that he must have the wrong Andrew, that I'm Andrew, ... uh, Andrew ... Smith. I'll just use my character's name. Why not?" Marshall smiled at the idea. "It could get to be an interesting conversation if he just sticks to general topics. Maybe it'll teach him to be very careful next time he dials his friend Andrew's number."

With that, he went back to the Phillies box score until his agent, Duane, called. He talked business with him for a while, then prepared to go out to a movie that he'd been wanting to see. Something about mistaken identities.

The cellphone chimed.

He had started out the door and was tempted to not answer, but it suddenly occurred to him it might be the same caller from before. He decided that now was as good a time as any to get that mix-up settled, and he answered the phone on his way to the car.

"Hello."

"Hello, is Andrew there?"

"Yes, this is Andrew." He smiled to himself.

"Andrew Smith?"

He gasped in surprise. That is what he was supposed to say and his subconscious let out a startled "Yes!" before he realized what he was saying.

"Andrew, my name is Osbourne Smith. You know, I have a brother named Andrew, too. In fact, he's with me right now." There was a pause. "We've been looking for you for a long time, Andrew. A very long time."

Marshall couldn't speak for a moment and barely managed to find his voice. "What, what do you want?"

"Right now, all we wanted was to hear you admit that you are Andrew Smith, and that you're there. We'll be getting in touch with you again just a little later. For tonight, go out and enjoy yourself. But don't try to run.

We've looked for you for a long time and we're not about to let you disappear. Good night. Pleasant dreams."

The call ended.

Marshall took the phone away from his ear and stood there staring at it for several minutes. Then he desperately tried to laugh.

"George. It had to be George. Either him or Duane. They must have put someone up to it. They're the only ones that knew about the Smith brothers. It had to be one of them."

But he wasn't sure. Not really. There had been something about the caller's voice that didn't sound like a practical joke. The caller had been too calm, too sure of himself, to be kidding. Besides, he realized, George and Duane weren't the kind to pull a trick like this – to scare a man half to death.

Marshall went out for the evening and tried to enjoy the movie. But his dreams that night weren't very pleasant at all.

The next morning was uneventful, but the phone calls from the previous day had so unnerved him that he still wasn't able to come up with a good death for the last Andrew Smith. He went to lunch, still brooding over it, hoping that Glass could help him with it. But Glass was preoccupied with other customers and he came back from his meal, still unsure about what to write.

He sat at his desk for an hour before he finally decided that there was no new special way to kill this Andrew Smith. The thing to do was to disguise Smith and let him escape from the brothers. Maybe he could write a sequel with them looking for him again. Make two books out of the story.

He finished the story and settled back with a sigh of relief. There was still a lot of rewriting to do, but he knew what he was doing now.

The cellphone chimed.

He reached for it slowly, wondering if he should answer it at all. He was tempted to let it ring until it stopped, but yesterday it had kept ringing until he finally answered it.

"Hello?"

"Hello, Andrew."

"No, ... no, I'm not! There isn't any Andrew here! You must have the wrong number!" He reached for the button to end the call.

"Andrew, don't hang up. We know it's you, Andrew. This isn't any wrong number. We only have the one. And we recognize your voice by now." There was a pause. "Andrew, we've waited too long. Almost the entire book. We can't let you go now. We're going to kill you. You're the last one, Andrew. The last one." The caller sighed. "You don't know what it means to finally get it over with. We've been looking for you for so long. You're not going to escape from us again. Not like you did the first time. There's no disguise for you now that we can't spot. You have one hour to live. Exactly one hour. You will receive the final call then. That will give you enough time to say your goodbyes. I hope your will is in order. Goodbye, Mr. Andrew Smith."

The call ended.

Marshall hit End, and spoke out loud, as if to reassure himself. "I suppose I should be scared. Worried anyway. I should try to run – but it doesn't frighten me now. In one hour, this thing is going to be settled, one way or another." He took a deep breath. "I have no real regrets, no loved ones to leave. I even got my last book done, though no sequel. Duane will find it. If I die, it may even become a bestseller." He looked at his laptop open on his desk. He stared at it for a long time, then laughed out loud.

"I did it! It's the ending I gave it! He escapes from them! That's what did it! If I had killed him, then it would have been over with. But they had to keep looking for him and they had to have an Andrew Smith to find."

As he looked at the laptop, a thought occurred to him. "Maybe it's not too late. I haven't printed out my last chapter yet. Maybe I can change it." He glanced at his watch, but he wasn't sure when the hour would end. Sitting down, he brought up his draft and deleted that last chapter. He started typing again, this time intending to rewrite his history.

The cellphone chimed.

He ignored it. He wasn't done yet. He needed more time. The chiming stopped. He continued writing for his life.

The cellphone chimed.

He continued typing. Just a little more time. Just a few more minutes. The phone stopped.

There was a knocking at the back door. No, they're here. He could hear the door start to open behind him.

He finished typing.

On the page, it read, "*Andrew Smith pulled the trigger. The other Andrew rocked for a few seconds, then fell, joining the body of his dead brother on the floor. Their long bloody quest was over.*"

Marshall slowly turned to look at the door. It was half open. Rising, he went to the door and looked outside, but no one was there. He picked up his phone and released a long breath. *I think I'm going to get a new number, just in case.*

If ... you get a chance to break away from one of those interminable meetings at your state conference, and are able to spend some time with one of your fellow attendees, maybe you should listen to his story .... Maybe it might be more interesting than any of the meetings ....

COMING HOME

Wingate doesn't come to the state conferences any more.

I think the company got tired of sending him if he wasn't going to go to any actual meetings. You can get away with hiding out in the bar for the whole three days, maybe once, maybe twice. But not for the six years that Wingate apparently did. But, I also now know there's more to it than that.

I met him at my first, and presumably his last, conference. I'd been to as many presentations as I thought I could handle for one day and had stopped in the hotel bar for a drink, and to see if I could find any of my similarly-thinking colleagues. Wingate spotted my obligatory nametag and waved me over. For somebody new like me, he was a virtual fountain of information about big names from the state organization, spouting out tales and scandalous rumors.

"The only reason Sanderson is here is to check out new blood to take under her wing," he winked, "and into her bed. I'd watch out for her if I were you. Boliero presents every year just to get away from his wife. He hasn't had anything new to say in literally years. Hopkins is good. She knows her stuff and is funny."

I nodded. I had just been to her workshop. "Do you know anything about this Ben Lloyd that's talking tomorrow? There seems to be a lot of mystery about him. Apparently, he used to be a big name in the business, but disappeared for a few years and everyone's anxious to find out what happened."

Wingate leaned back and just sat for a minute, tapping the table with his finger. "Yes, I know. I plan to be there tomorrow, too."

He seemed to want to add to that, so I simply took a long drink and waited.

Wingate looked back up at me. "Do you have to be anywhere in the next hour or so?" When I shook my head, he continued, "It's probably about time I told someone, anyway. You didn't know him, so maybe, just maybe, you'll listen with an open mind."

I listened as he shared his story.

########

First of all, completely disappearing is not something that anyone would ever have expected of him. Ben Lloyd was always a strong personality. He knew what he wanted, and he knew how to get it. It wasn't ruthlessness. He did care about people, but sometimes that didn't make any difference.

He and I were not really friends, but we knew each other well enough to get together at these conferences and have dinner. I enjoyed doing that because I could go back to the office the next week and say, "When I was talking with Ben Lloyd ...", and it would boost my status a bit ... and justify my coming back the next year. At least I liked to think so. I do think he also enjoyed showing off to someone and being thought of as a sort of mentor.

I'm sure he did the same thing with other 'lesser lights' at each meeting, but he was fascinating to talk to, and it was usually the highlight of the week for me.

Anyway, it was about six years ago that I last saw him.

We had run into each other earlier in the day and had set a time for dinner. He was being interviewed for the local paper – the conference that year was in the city he had grown up in, the same city as this year – so we didn't get away till probably about seven o'clock.

He had been his usual positive, smiling self for the reporter, but he grabbed my arm as we left the hotel and pulled me around to face him. I had never seen him look so worried.

"Look, Wingate, you've known me for several years. How do I look to you?"

"You look fine." I didn't know what he was worried about, but it sure couldn't have been with how he looked. "As a matter of fact, I've never seen you look better. You look ten years younger than the last time I saw you."

"Damn." That certainly wasn't the sort of response I was expecting. "You're the third person to tell me that today."

"So, what's the problem?"

He exploded. "Because you're right! I look and feel like I did when I was thirty. Only I'm forty-two."

"I'd like to know your secret." I smiled.

He didn't smile back. "So would I. I haven't done anything. Yesterday, I still looked forty-two, at least. Since I arrived in town last night, I've lost fifteen pounds and I don't feel the pain I've had in my knee for the last five years."

I still didn't take him seriously. "I always told my boss that I needed these conferences to rejuvenate me, but you're taking it to extremes. Come on, let's go all out on dinner and I'm sure you'll gain that weight back."

But dinner didn't work. If anything, he seemed to get thinner and younger. He kept looking at his hands and running his fingers through his hair. I wasn't sure, but the hair seemed to have gotten thicker and longer.

######

Wingate stopped and looked at his empty glass. I got the message and came back with refills.

"What was it – a magic drug? A trick?"

Wingate sipped at his drink, muttered, "It's stranger than that," and continued.

######

After dinner, we walked back in the direction of the hotel. I was having trouble keeping up with Ben's energetic pace, when he suddenly stopped and stared at a storefront across the street.

"I know that place," he pointed. "There's something about …"

He crossed the street, and I had to hurry again to catch up.

"Meyer's Books. Something about Meyer's Books." He turned to me. "Did you ever experience déjà vu, Wingate? That's what I'm, … only it's so strong. There's something there that I used to know. I know it. Come on, before it closes."

With anyone else, I would have suspected some trick, a practical joke. But I'd been watching him physically change before my eyes. And practical jokes just weren't Ben Lloyd's style.

There were only a few customers browsing. And, to my mind, they seemed old-fashioned, both in clothing and behavior. Which fit the store, which seemed to be mostly a collection of classics and early editions. I didn't recognize anything from the recent bestseller lists.

Ben reached out to some of the bindings, seeming to draw an electrical charge from each touch – seeming to grow younger still.

Toward one side, a few overstuffed chairs were set aside, apparently for customers to sit in to read at their leisure. Ben sat in one of the chairs, gingerly at first, then relaxed back and closed his eyes.

"This is where I used to sit." He turned and draped his legs over an arm of the chair. "With my legs like this. And read. And read. This was my favorite place in the whole world. How could I ever have forgotten this?"

He pointed to the wall opposite.

"There's the Tom Sawyer print! And next to it is one of the Three Musketeers. I used to look at those for hours and dream myself into those adventures."

I wasn't sure what was going on. There were times and places from my youth that I remembered with fondness, but I was usually aware of when I might come upon them. I could only guess that it surprised him that the bookstore was still here.

He must have finally noticed my puzzled expression.

"Wingate, you don't know about my past, do you?" He motioned for me to sit in a chair opposite him. "Well, nobody does." I sat, not knowing where he was going with this, but fascinated by the possibilities.

"I don't know where to start. I suppose, from where I can." He took a deep breath. "I spent my teenage years in a series of foster homes. I was lucky in that I had foster parents who kept me focused on working hard to get a better life. Before the foster homes, I was briefly in an orphanage. And before that, nothing. Nothing anyway, but vague images of yelling, and police, and lots of kids. Very chaotic." He gestured toward the books. "And now this. I had forgotten this place. I used to spend a lot of time here."

He turned back to me. "I don't remember my early childhood. And I never really wanted to. I never made any effort to go back and try to find out anything."

He suddenly swung his legs around and sat up straight.

"There's Meyer!" He pointed excitedly at an elderly man at the register. "I don't believe it. He must be ... but he doesn't look any older than I remember. It has to be thirty years!"

"Maybe it's his son." But, as I said it, I didn't believe it. Lloyd no longer looked like the mature man I had known. He looked to be about twenty now and, for the first time, I became scared, really scared, of whatever might happen next.

Lloyd stood up and moved toward the counter. I had no choice but to follow.

"Mr. Meyer?"

"Yes?" The man seemed about seventy. I couldn't see him either losing or adding thirty years and still looking the same. He paused for a second, and raised a finger to point at Lloyd.

"Wait, ... Benjy? It is you! Oh, my. It's good to see you. I haven't seen you in, what, eight or nine years?"

Eight or nine years. Lloyd had said thirty. Somewhere we had lost over twenty years.

"You're looking good, Benjy. I almost didn't recognize you."

"You look the same, Mr. Meyer. You haven't changed at all."

"What's there to change? Once an old fossil, always an old fossil." Meyer grinned. "But what about you? How have you been? I knew the agency had taken you out of your home, but I haven't heard anything since." His grin faded. "I hope life has been good to you."

Lloyd gripped the counter hard and shut his eyes for a second. A dark cloud seemed to pass over his face.

"Things have been ... better. The people I've been with have been good to me. I've been to college. I think everything's going to be okay from now on."

"That's good, Benjy. That's real good. I've thought about you often. I always knew you had it in you. You were the Lloyd that would make it."

"Mr. Meyer, I've been gone a long time. Do you know what has happened to the rest of my family?"

'Well, your mother still lives there, as far as I know. And Josie's with her. Pete's around, and sees her from time to time. Last I heard, he was working at the Ryson plant, but, to be honest, the rumor is he's been mixed up in some illegal stuff on the side." Meyer paused again. "Are you sure you want to hear all this?" Lloyd nodded. "Jack ran away from home about four years ago and I haven't heard from him since. The agency took Sandra out within a year after you left. She was in and out of foster homes. She got them to bring her back here once or twice, but it's been a long time now."

Lloyd clenched and unclenched his hands at his side. "Damn. I should have stayed."

Meyer put his hand on Lloyd's shoulder. "There wasn't anything you could do. You were just a kid. And it would have killed you, too. One way or another. You had to leave for you to have a chance." Lloyd tapped his fingers on the counter. His whole body tightened for a moment, then abruptly relaxed. A ghost of a smile appeared.

"You're right, Mr. Meyer. I had to leave. But now, I think it's time for me to go home."

"Benjy, you have to take care of yourself. You've got too much ahead of you. Don't go back to that life."

"It's okay, Mr. Meyer, really. I'm going to be fine. I mean it." He took a deep breath. "I'm not going to lose my future. I'm just going to reclaim some of my past."

He turned and started toward the door. Meyer called him back.

"Wait. I've been keeping something for you." He reached under the counter and pulled out a bag. "Here. These were your favorite books. I've been saving them. Just in case. You know."

"Thanks. For everything." Lloyd glanced inside the bag. "I'm sorry it took me so long to say that. You'll never know how much you, and this place, meant to me."

I had stayed quiet – not understanding, but not wanting to interrupt the moment.

Outside, Lloyd stopped for a moment, then pointed to the left. "It's just a few blocks away. Are you still with me, Wingate?"

"Ben, what's going on? I don't understand any of this."

"I don't know. Well, that's not quite true. I didn't know for a long, long time. But I think I do know now, and I hope I know why. I have to say I don't know how, but I don't care." He shrugged. "I would appreciate it if you'd walk with me, though."

We moved in the direction he'd indicated. As we walked, more years continued to quickly pass away from him.

"I would guess I'm in my late teens now. And I'm remembering more. As we get closer to my home, I'll probably get younger yet."

I almost stopped walking at that comment, but figured I was with him. Come what may.

"I was born in this city, but I haven't been back since I was a teenager. I never even thought about coming back and, to be honest, I never even thought about the fact that the conference was here. It was just another city.

"Pete was, is, my older brother, by about three years. Sandra is my twin sister. God, to have not thought about her in thirty years. We used to be so close. Jack's two years younger and Josie four years younger than that.

"We were poor. My parents worked odd jobs and had no real skills to go beyond that. Dad was a drunk and beat us whenever the mood hit. My mom let it happen. Back then, the wife didn't argue with the husband – the supposedly 'good old days' – but she was even weaker than that. In order to stay out of the way of my dad's fists, she'd use one of us as a shield."

I shuddered at the thought, but was aware that it was all too common an occurrence.

"When I was about twelve years old, my mom sent me to get my dad out of a bar at about two in the morning. He had a rare chance to earn some money the next day, and she didn't want him to blow it. I came upon him in an alley, arguing with another drunk from the bar. I don't know who started it, but soon they were shoving and threatening each other. One of them pulled out a knife, then the other one did. It ended up with the other drunk stabbing and killing my dad."

Lloyd stopped briefly, remembering the vividness of the moment, then moved on.

"I was too afraid to run. And too afraid to yell. I just stood there, and eventually the man noticed me. I suppose he could have killed me then and there, but he didn't. He just threatened me, and told me I had better forget that I had ever seen anything.

"I forgot so well that I forgot everything. I withdrew so much that the agency took me away. And I never came back."

By now, Lloyd looked to be close to that twelve years old. He was just a scared boy again. But he was no longer hiding behind a blank memory.

"Wingate, I've been a success. I got away from here and I made it. Now I need to go back and help them. I'm twelve years old in body, but forty-two in experience. I know what needs to be done and how to do it. How this happened, I don't know, but I have to take advantage of it – to recapture my childhood and to save my family."

"Are you going to turn in the guy that killed your father?" I was stunned, but looking for something to say.

Lloyd shook his head. "No, either one could have died. There's no one to help with that. It's my brothers and sisters that I'm here for. It's their future, not their past."

We had stopped in front of a brownstone.

"It's just up those steps. First apartment on the left."

"Why am I here, Ben?"

He clapped me on the shoulder, an odd gesture from a twelve-year-old. "I think you're here just to help me get this far. And maybe, for someone to know what happened." He pointed back down the street. "If you go back this way, you should eventually find the hotel. Once back there, I suspect it will be the right time again for you. Here," he pulled one of the books out of the bag, "take this and think of me when you read it. Maybe I'll have to grow up again. Maybe I won't."

He went up the stairs and through the front door. I waited a few moments, but he didn't reappear. It was then that I looked at the book he had given me. *Peter Pan* by James Barrie. The boy who stayed a boy forever.

######

Once Wingate had finished, I just sat in silence for a few minutes. There wasn't much one could say. Eventually I asked him, "Did you read the book?"

"Some of it. I already knew the story. At that moment, I think Lloyd saw himself as the eternal youth protecting the other children from the evils of the world. I don't know.

"When I saw he was presenting tomorrow, I tried to find him. But he's not registered at the hotel and no one seems to know where he is."

He stood up. "I know. You've probably got so many questions that you don't know which one to ask first. But I don't have any answers. I'd suggest that you come to the workshop tomorrow and we'll see what we'll see." With that, he left.

I didn't know what to think of Wingate's story. It certainly seemed too fantastic to be true. Maybe it was just something they tried on newcomers to the conference. Whatever, there was certainly no way I was going to miss that presentation.

I got there early. In fact, I skipped the meeting before it just to make sure. Wingate wasn't there yet. Only a college kid was there posting a sign at the door. When I got close enough, I could read that Ben Lloyd's workshop had been canceled.

"What happened?"

The young man just shrugged. "Maybe he had something better to do." He turned to pick up a bag from the floor. "Like me. I'm going to a ballgame with my sister and a friend I haven't seen in several years." He turned to leave.

"Wait. Can't you tell me anything about why it's canceled? I really needed to meet Mr. Lloyd."

"Maybe he just wasn't … ready. Maybe he needed more time. Tell you what."

He reached into his bag. "Read this and maybe it will help." He handed me a book and walked toward the elevator.

I stared at his back for a moment, then looked down at the book. It was *The Time Machine* by H. G. Wells.

I hurried after the boy, but the elevator doors were just closing as I got there. However, the gap was open enough for me to see him show ballgame tickets to a girl who looked just like him … and Wingate.

If ... the local clothing recycling bin appeared to be haunted, and if ... your town wanted someone to investigate, wouldn't Dr. Hiram McBottom seem the logical choice?

AND SO THE CROCODILE SANG

Once upon a time .... Well, actually, it wasn't once upon a time. As a matter of fact, it was just the other day, you know, just around the bend into last week. But "once upon a time" tends to immediately catch a reader's attention, and it has such a ring of authenticity and authority about it. But we digress ... on to last week.

It was a day like most of the others that had been recently beaming upon Bottomsburg, typical early May. The trees were beginning to clothe themselves again, and the flowers were letting loose with a big yawn after the long winter. Not a cloud in the sky and no reason for any to be on the fresh, shiny faces of the villagers.

Mrs. Warmbottom was making her annual pilgrimage to the clothing charity bin down at the corner. Once a year, she would collect all the old worthless junk and the outgrown clothes that lay around the house, whether or not Mr. Warmbottom was done wearing them, or was actually still wearing them at the time, and, instead of bothering the trashman with such utterly worthless stuff, would give it to the charity people and let them worry about it.

So, off she went with the usual relief at getting rid of such a troublesome clutter in her house, though she did still have to deal with Mr. Warmbottom.

No one ever knew for a certainty what it was that specifically made her come screaming home, leaving her precious junk strewn the entire length of the road. Whether it was the raven that sat on top of the bin and quoth, "Nevermore", or the voice that came from within, "Buzzy, how many times have I told you to be less, ... dramatic? If there is someone coming, just simply say, 'Someone is coming'", or both, she never said.

If there was more to this strange conversation, Mrs. Warmbottom never heard it. Her screams could have wakened the dead, as many pale townspeople afterwards claimed they did. Word spread quickly as to what had happened, the quickness primarily due to Mrs. Warmbottom's neighbor, old Mrs. Coldbottom, the town gossip. A crowd soon gathered around the charity bin, nobody daring to go too near it, content to stand and watch the Raven scratch himself. Murmurings passed through the gathering, all the sorts of things that people say to each other at a time like that.

"Did you hear about ...?"

"Well, I'll be ..."

"She said it had a voice like that movie, ..."

"You don't say ..."

"I heard that it was much worse than that ..."

As I said, all the sorts of things that people say to each at a time like that. As if there were times like that.

That very night, a town meeting was called by Mayor Bottom to discuss the issue, and every single inhabitant of Bottomsburg turned out for it. All the Bottoms—the old Bottoms and the young Bottoms, the big Bottoms and the wee Bottoms, all came to the meeting.

Comments flew from all sides – questions as to who had brought the charity bin into town originally, on whose property did it stand, and who was the last person to discard anything into it. All very important questions. But nobody waited to hear any answers. Blame was being put on everybody and everybody was putting blame on somebody, without much getting settled.

Mayor Bottom rapped his gavel for quiet.

"Order, order! We have to have order!"

The mayor looked around in surprise at the sudden peace that had descended upon the crowd.

"Good people of Bottomsburg, fellow Bottoms, we are gathered here to discuss a problem of supreme importance. It has come to the attention of this office that, ... um ...."

The mayor was a well-loved figure, but he had a terrible memory, particularly for names and problems of supreme importance. He referred to his notes and continued.

"That, uh, mysterious incidents have been occurring at the charity bin on West Cheek Road. There are reports of a mysterious bird and a mysterious voice." He looked up. "Does anybody have any ideas on how to contend with these? Yes, Mr. Bluebottom?"

The bewhiskered elderly editor of the town paper, The Bottomsburg Burp (you were expecting something else?), rose and cleared his throat.

"The most qualified investigation, I should assume, for these proceedings, hmph, would be the logical choice for undertaking to study the aviary phenomenon before us. In other words, the winged creature atop the receptacle, the obviously ravenous raven, the bird. So, hemph, without further deliberation, I should suggest, we turn this matter over to the eminent, well-known president of the local chapter of the Billy Bob Featherbottom Bird-Watching Society, Dr. ... (Mr. Bluebottom was blessed with a memory every bit as outstanding as the Mayor's) ..., Dr. ... Hiram McBottom, that's it, Dr. Hiram McBottom."

The applause was deafening, for if any Bottom was more beloved in Bottomsburg than all the other Bottoms, it was old beloved Dr. Hiram McBottom. He had made his fortune in his youth by building a popular chain of quick-service (rather than fast food) hamburger stands, but had then gone back to his first love, watching. In his much, much younger days it had been female-watching, but age had caught up to him and he had gone on to bird-watching (still actually the same activity in Great Britain), which was much easier on his heart. He had made a special study of the whippoorwill terwilligers, which nobody else but he had ever seen. He was also one of the very few individuals alive that could tell the difference between a female yellow-tufted, blue-beaked, green-breasted rednik and a male yellow-tufted, blue-beaked, green-breasted rednik. And he was the only one still outside of an asylum.

Dr. McBottom stood immobile for several hours, watching the bird. Not that he was so utterly fascinated with it (he had long ago decided that it was either a raven or a hairy bald eagle), but once he had arranged himself into a certain position, it was extremely hard for him to move out of it again. The raven, for his part, was utterly fascinated with the doctor, attempting to determine if he was sleeping or had taken root.

The doctor finally broke the silence. "Well, don't just sit there, do something." The raven promptly did. "I don't mean that. That, I assume you can do. That, any bird can do. I'm Dr. McBottom. They tell me you talk, or, more precisely, you can say 'Nevermore' in very dramatic tones. Poe to the contrary, I have never yet been able to find a raven who could do that, and I sincerely doubt that you will prove to be the exception."

"Maybe you just haven't been looking in the right places for talking ravens. After all, they aren't just another common everyday bird," the raven quoth.

The doctor nodded. "It could be. It could very well be. I haven't been everywhere, and there are many sights that I have never seen, but ...." It suddenly dawned on him whose remark he was responding to, "You spoke! You talked to me! You exist!"

"Of course I exist. Was there ever any doubt about that?"

"I mean you actually exist as a talking bird! I didn't believe it could possibly be, and yet here you are talking to me."

Here the good doctor, rather surprisingly, broke into song.

"I didn't believe it could possibly be,
Yet here you are talking to me.
Where do you come from? Where have you been?
Why are you something that I've never seen?
They told me you didn't, you couldn't exist.
What will they say when I tell them of this?
Your voice is so deep, from deep down below,

They must believe when I tell them it's so.
The words that you speak, the things that you say,
As a watcher of birds, this must be my day.
A raven who talks, who says 'Nevermore',
Then goes back and says what he didn't before.
So many strange things that I have just heard,
You wouldn't believe that they came from a bird.
I didn't believe it could possibly be,
Yet here you are, talking to me."

The raven clapped his wings as well as wings could be clapped. "Bravo, nevermore, I mean, very good! That's the greatest imitation of a whippoor-will terwilliger that I have ever heard!"

Dr. McBottom burst out once more.

"I didn't believe it could possibly be,
Yet here you are, talking to me."

"Oh, you weren't done." The raven ruffled his feathers back into shape, then waited a few seconds to ensure the completion of the song.

"Finished? Okay. I feel I ought to introduce myself. My name is, was, Thomas 'Buzzy' Bearnstein. I used to be a man like, well, I don't want to say like yourself, but I was formerly a man. There wasn't any wicked witch or evil stepmother who turned me into a raven as a curse or anything like that. The simple truth is I died, and chose to be reincarnated as a raven.

"My friend in the box below, whose voice, I'm afraid frightened that poor lady, has not yet decided what he wants to come back as and that is why we are here. He wants to look around a bit before he decides, and I have been chosen to be his guide because I was a friend of his during his life." Buzzy scratched at the top of the bin.

"Come on out, Chumley. His name is George Ivan Chumley, and he's very shy. Don't be scared now when you first see him. He is in the form of what you people would call a ghost. We prefer to think of it as a distorted previous manifestation. Come on, Chumley, he's waiting."

The good doctor could hear rustling from the interior of the bin. Then the lid slowly rose. And a face became framed in the opening.

G. I. Chumley smiled at the doctor, "Howdy, Doc, how's tricks? Sorry we had to put you through this, but we didn't know how else to make ourselves known. As a brand spanking-new ghost, I'm not too good at walking around in broad daylight yet. And, unless you're prepared, Buzzy, here likes to be too mysterious, if you know what I mean, to be accepted without at least a flicker of the eyelids. Well, now that you're here, Doc, got any ideas on a good life for someone to be?"

"Mr. Chumley ..."

"Call me George. No one else does, but you can be the first, Doc. First in hamburgers, first in terwilligers, and first to call me George. Hey, that's pretty good, isn't it, Buzzy? Tell George Washington, next flock of bald eagles you see him in, that he can use it. It's all his."

Buzzy pulled a notebook out from somewhere under a back wing and made a note of it.

"Not too bad, uh, George, especially the parts about the hamburgers and terwilligers." Dr. McBottom responded. "But now back to the matter at hand ..., uh, would you mind stepping outside? The lid keeps flapping in your face and distracting me."

"I'm sorry, Doc, but this is all there is of me right now. Just my head. The rest won't appear till later, they tell me. I'm setting on top of an old tennis racket right now," Chumley shrugged what little there was of his shoulders.

"Well, I suppose that's alright, then. Now, about finding a good life."

"Mr. Chumley, uh, George, you seem to be under the impression that you can find some kind of life that can be classified as good before it even begins. It doesn't work that way.

"Take any kind of life, they all have their inborn problems. A chicken has to worry if the trouble and time it takes for him to travel across a road will be worth it when she reaches the other side. A crocodile can't express his happiness because he can't sing. A lion, that majestic king of the forest, must always be ready to defend his title. A worm worries about where the next bird is going to come from, the bird worries about where the next worm will be. And man, man is worst of all because he has only himself and his fellow kind to fear. And those he can't avoid. The only good life is one that you, yourself, make good.

"I can't tell you what life to choose any more than I can tell you what makes a good life. All I can tell you is what hamburger to eat, because I can tell you what it takes to make a good burger. And the best hamburger is a 'Big Bottom'. So, my advice is to go out and have one today, even if you don't deserve a break, because I need the money.

"But choose your own life, and do with it what you can. Be a speedy chicken, be a mighty lion, be a singing crocodile, but be it.

"That's all I can say to you, George," the doctor turned to Buzzy. "But you, a talking raven, huh? You're quite a phenomenon, you know. You ever think of making some money, touring the world, seeing the inside of a cage ...?"

"And that's the entire story. Mayor Bottom," Dr. McBottom finished up. "That's why they were in the charity bin."

"The town thanks you for your pugnacity and your perseverance in pursuing this problem, Doctor. Then we have nothing further to fear from our feathered friend and the faux face?" The mayor leaned back in his chair. "But what are they doing now? Have they left town yet? Last I heard, the bin was still occupied."

"It is, your honor, sir. I've arranged with the charities for the bird and the ghost to temporarily reside there. This Chumley still wants to look around before deciding what to become. I have also gotten them both jobs with the Greater Bottomsburg Zoo. Buzzy will be with other aviary creatures, doing group therapy, I believe, and George is trying to teach the crocodile to sing and the chicken to run more quickly. I rather get the feeling that if anybody can do it, he can. You never know ..."

An unexpected consequence of Chumley and Buzzy taking over the charity bin as their temporary abode was the reluctance of Bottomsburg wives to dispose of their unwanted or unneeded old clothing and otherwise unnecessary junk in that bin. There was a lot of "You take it," "No, it's your turn," You won't catch me near there," going around the neighborhood. Homes were beginning to fill up with piles of outgrown or outdated articles of clothes.

It wasn't until after the last thaw in early spring that Mr. Warmbottom was finally discovered still sitting in his favorite easy chair under a growing heap of what used to be, in his much younger years, his well-worn sweaters. He seemed none the worse for wear.

AS I WAS OUT WALKING THE BOG

As I was out walking the bog
I wisht I was walking me dog.
The mist was becoming a fog
I was needing to sit on a log
As I was out walking the bog.

As I was out walking the fen
I wisht I was walking me hen.
I've thought of it now and again
I wisht I had thought of it then
As I was out walking the fen.

As I was out walking the marsh
I wisht I was walking me horse.
I know it sounds silly, of course
To be walking, not riding me horse
As I was out walking the marsh.

As I was out walking the flats
I wisht I was walking me cats.
The wind would have blown off their hats
And that would, of course, have been that
As I was out walking the flats.

As I was out walking the road
I wisht I was walking me toad.
He would have croaked, but not crowed
And could have helped carry me load
As I was out walking the road.

As I was out walking the trail
I wisht I was walking me snail.
I wouldn't have stepped on its tail
She could have come up in me pail
As I was out walking the trail.

As I was out walking the lake
I wisht I was walking me snake.
It would have been real, not fake
Though it could have been easy to make
As I was out walking the lake.

As I was out walking the bog
I wisht I was walking me dog
And me hen and me horse and me cats
And me toad and me snail and me snake
As I was out walking the bog.

If ... your elevator seems to be taking a long time to reach its destination, and is stopping frequently with no one else getting on, would you start to worry? After all, elevators have been known to stop working. At least the way you want them to.

THE MAN ON THE 13TH FLOOR

Kennedy closed the office door behind him and locked it. The hour was late, and he walked silently down the hall past the rest of the now-dark offices to the elevator doors and pressed the down button. After waiting a moment, the thought crossed his mind (as it had so many times before) that the elevators just took too damn long to get here. He would rather have walked down if it wasn't for the fact that he worked on the nineteenth floor.

In the midst of his reverie, the doors finally opened. He stepped into the empty elevator and pushed the button for the lobby. The doors shut with a particularly ominous thunk that struck him as different somehow.

He glanced at his watch, saw that it was 7:37, and frowned, wondering if his supper would still be warm when he got home.

The elevator slowed to a stop and opened its doors. Kennedy began to move forward, then realized that it wasn't the lobby he was stepping out into. He looked up at the floor indicator and saw that the number 13 was lit up. It struck Kennedy as strange because he didn't recall there being a thirteenth floor in the building. He had never noticed a button for it before, simply thought that the numbers jumped from 12 to 14. He had assumed that this building, like a lot of other similar structures, had eliminated the superstitious thirteenth.

Stepping back into the elevator, he glanced around the floor. It appeared to him to be the same as the other floors, except that it was exceptionally clean and new looking. A young boy, maybe five years old, was standing outside the door staring at him. Kennedy was about to ask him if he was going to get on or not when the elevator doors closed between them. Now closed silently, he noticed.

Kennedy shrugged off the elevator's stopping and opening as a young child's curiosity with buttons. The boy must have pushed one, wondering what would happen, and must have been surprised when an older man started to step out from behind the doors.

But then, the young boy must have used the elevator to get up to the thirteenth floor. Maybe he had just wanted to go down to the lobby, but had become afraid to get into the elevator with a stranger. That actually made sense, he thought.

The elevator continued its silent journey.

It seemed to have gone down only a few more flights when it stopped again. Kennedy tapped his foot in impatience but stopped when he noticed which button was lit up. His expression was first one of puzzlement, then turned to one of mild frustration as the doors of the elevator opened out again onto the thirteenth floor.

A young man, maybe twenty years old, was standing in front of the doors, staring at him. Kennedy just stared back as the youth made no move to step onto the elevator. He thought he noticed a slight smile on the more-than-familiar face as the doors closed again.

Kennedy remained staring at the closed doors as the elevator continued downward, confused by what had happened. There had been no button curiosity or fear of strangers involved here. The young man had simply not wanted to get on. For the first time, a twinge of anxiety rose within him.

There were other things that nibbled at the back of his brain. On the elevator's previous stop, what had really stood out in Kennedy's mind was the newness and spotlessness of the hall as compared to others. It had even smelled new. But this time, the floor had appeared a bit dirtier. He couldn't put his finger on it, but he had the impression that the thirteenth floor had aged more than a few seconds between the first and second stops.

Though the little boy hadn't been visible, Kennedy had the distinct impression that he had been there. The young man actually had looked like one would have expected the boy to look at about that age. Maybe they were brothers. Though there was something that stirred more familiarity than that, Kennedy was willing to assume that was what he was recognizing.

He had just gotten that settled in his mind, and his heart had started to beat normally again when the elevator stopped. Kennedy tried to keep from looking at the floor number, but he couldn't resist and raised his head. He gasped and started in the beginnings of fearful anticipation as the doors slid open again on the thirteenth floor.

A middle-aged man, maybe forty years old, was standing outside the doors looking straight into his eyes, with another slight smile on his face. Kennedy prayed that the man, whom he immediately recognized as a virtual image of himself at that age, wouldn't get on this time either. Beads of sweat had broken out on his forehead, but he heaved a sigh of relief when the doors closed and the man was still on the other side.

Kennedy wondered how long this was going to go on as he tried to keep his mind off the resemblance between the boy, the youth, and the older man, as well as now himself. There was also the further aging of the hallway. The lights were dim, but paint was starting to peel and the carpeting showed signs of dirt. Thinking of the length of time passing, he lifted his wrist for the first time since he had entered the elevator. He stared in shock at his watch and shook it vigorously, but the time didn't change. It was 7:37. Only a few seconds had elapsed since he had been standing on the nineteenth floor.

His perspiration was building, and he frantically pushed all the floor buttons on the board. He had an instant's sensation of relief when the elevator slowed, then shuddered as he saw the same number light up.

This time, a much older man, possibly eighty years old, was standing there. Behind him was a dark and dusty hallway with cobwebs on every corner. Kennedy prayed, this time, that the old man would get on and end whatever was going to happen. He didn't think that he could take any more strain on his heart.

The old man, an elderly version of the three previous appearances, smiled at Kennedy and boarded the elevator.

Kennedy now had some inkling of what was happening and, unsurprisingly, heard the snap of the elevator cables above him, feeling the car begin to pick up speed. He arranged his clothing in an orderly fashion in an attempt to remain dignified, and turned to the old man, speaking calmly and with a wry smile on his face.

"I think I understand. Death is the man waiting on the thirteenth floor."

If ... you are visiting the land known for its many vortexes (yes, vortexes, not vortices), and you are offered the opportunity to explore the most mysterious one of all, one very few people know about, would you do it? Not knowing how it might turn out?

VORTEX OF THE LOST WOLF

As Aaron and Julie Bridges pulled their rental car into the restaurant parking lot for what they thought was an early morning breakfast, Julie exclaimed, "Oh, no, I don't see a parking spot. Can we go around and try to get into that plaza next door?"

"Wait a minute." Aaron suddenly stopped, looked back to make sure there was no one behind him, and reversed the car for a few feet. "I think there's one about to leave."

A family of four was moving to both sides of a minivan and opening the doors. The boy and girl started arguing over which side they wanted to sit on, but the dad gave them just one "dad" look, and they got in quickly. The mom pulled out a map before she swung into the passenger side, and Aaron hung his head in slight exasperation. As he feared, the parents appeared to be taking a few moments to check where they wanted to go. But Aaron was not giving up his chance for this spot, and eventually the minivan backed up and got on its way.

"This had better be good," he said as he finally pulled into the spot.

"The concierge said The Coffeepot is the best breakfast in Sedona. Or at least the most choices. One hundred and one omelets. What more do you want?"

"Maybe one hundred and two, because it looks like they're serving each and every one of those one hundred and one right now." He was grimacing at the full lot and the line of people outside the door.

Julie took him by the arm. "We'll see what the wait time is. And one day or another, we're going to have a breakfast here. Look, we got lucky with the parking spot."

On their way to the door, they passed an older man in a flannel shirt under a windbreaker, with jeans and serious hiking boots. He looked like he was trying to talk a younger couple into something, but the younger male was shaking his head and the woman had just pulled out her cell phone, as if to check anything else.

"Sign in here and it will probably be ten minutes." The young woman at the desk was smiling, and it seemed to be a genuine smile.

"Really?" Aaron was having trouble believing it as he looked at the twenty people jammed into the waiting area. "Ten minutes?"

The woman shrugged. "More or less."

"That could cover a wide range of time," Aaron mumbled, but the smiling woman didn't hear, or at least pretended not to.

Julie pulled him into a corner that had just been vacated. "Ten minutes doesn't sound bad at all. Look at the pictures on the wall of famous people that have eaten here."

"Who the heck is ..." He peered closer at the signature. "Robert Mitchum? Or Slim Pickens? That's really his name?"

"I think they're old-time western actors. So," changing the subject, "what are we going to do today?"

"I know you want to see vortexes – you know it really should be vortices – but are there any we haven't yet seen? We've been to the Airport one, Cathedral Rock, Bell Rock, and the one canyon, Boynton, but I haven't felt anything yet."

Julie laughed. "But haven't you just felt the energy from being here in Sedona? And the views have been spectacular."

"Yeah, the views are great. They're so fantastic, they don't even look real. But I thought we were supposed to feel something. I don't know – uplifting, inspirational, at least something different. I can't say I've felt any of that energy they're always talking about."

"We could try shopping." Julie was enjoying the whole Sedona experience. "I know I always get energized from that."

"Excuse me." A voice came from Aaron's left and they looked up to find the older man from outside. "I don't mean to interrupt, but I couldn't help overhear that you were looking for vortexes."

Aaron cocked his head suspiciously, but Julie excitedly responded, "Oh, yes, we want to experience everything that we can while we're here."

"But not too expensive," Aaron added. "We can't afford the hot-air balloon or the helicopter rides. The stargazing was pretty much our limit."

"Oh, I'm not selling anything." The man put up his hand. "No, I just happen to know of a vortex that not too many other people know about, and I thought you might be interested in it. You said you're looking for a different kind of energy and I guarantee you will find it here.

"Let me write down the directions for you. It's not very far – on the way to Cottonwood." He pulled a pen from his pocket and tore out the next page from under the sign-in sheet. The smiling girl never paid him any attention. He scribbled a few lines down. "It's called Lost Wolf Vortex." He held out the paper and pen.

Aaron took both, and he and Julie looked down at the paper.

"Thank you, but that's okay. We may be going shopping today. And this afternoon might be a good time for just some relaxing and sitting out by the pool."

They looked back up, but the man was already gone. Aaron scanned the crowded room, but there was no sign of him.

"Bridges?" The woman at the counter was now smiling at them and waved for them to follow her. Their ten minutes were up, right on the dot.

######

"I have to admit, that was a pretty good breakfast. Bacon, onion, tomato, and sausage all together make a pretty filling omelet. And I'd even be willing to eat it again before we leave Sedona. Not right away, but maybe another day." Aaron pulled the car out onto the street. "Which way?"

"Go to the right." Julie was studying the piece of paper the mystery man had given them.

"I thought most of the shopping was the other direction?"

"I know, but we could do that this afternoon." She held up the paper. "This isn't very far. And what could it hurt?"

Aaron tightened his mouth. "I don't know. That guy seemed kind of weird. He was suddenly there, and then he was suddenly gone."

"Oh, come on. Weren't we supposed to be expecting some weirdness in Sedona? That's why we're here. He didn't try to sell us anything, which is different from other places." She now held up her phone. "I looked it up while you were in the bathroom. Lost Wolf Vortex does exist, but it's just mentioned in passing, as one of the mysteries of Sedona – hard to find and not well-known. But we've got the directions." She pointed to the paper.

Aaron shrugged. He rarely – okay, never – won a debate with his wife. "Alright, we'll have an adventure. Let's see where this takes us."

"It doesn't come up on our phone map, probably not well-known enough, but the first road, Grey Creek Drive, does. It should be about three miles on the left."

Just past the sign for Dead Horse Ranch – "Where the riding is easy" – they started looking for Grey Creek Drive. By squinting hard and slowing down at about the three-mile mark, they found the road and turned.

"Okay, now, we're looking for a fork in the road where Grey Creek continues to the right and, I think it says Grainy Creek, goes to the left. We take Grainy Creek."

"Boy, these names are all alike."

"I know, but I bet they always used geographical markers as names originally, and creeks were a good way to spot where you were. Here's the fork."

Aaron stopped the car, but they couldn't see a sign. There were two houses to the right and a car coming from the right fork. No apparent stop sign and the car just drove right by them.

Julie pointed to the left. "It says to take the left. It doesn't mention any other possible turns yet and my phone shows a road, but it doesn't give a name."

"Okay, it's your party." He made the turn. "Now where?"

They passed two houses on the left and a farm on the right. A car and a pickup truck passed them going the other way. They hadn't seen any other vehicles going in their direction.

"This says the second road to the right, and what looks like 'Gulley Creek'."

"Oh, come on."

"Well, it could be Galley Creek, or Golley Creek."

They eventually came to a dirt road. This time there was a big rock with Gulley Creek painted on it. Or it could have been Galley Creek or Golley Creek. The paint had smeared a little at some point.

"Are we sure we want to do this?" Aaron peered down the single-track road.

"We're almost there. It's only about a quarter-mile and then we'll be right in the middle of the vortex. I'd hate to go back now that we've come this far."

Aaron sighed and turned. "Well, at least the car's a rental if something happens."

After a few hundred yards, Julie noticed her cell phone read "No Reception", but she figured this was not the time to share that information with Aaron.

At just about the quarter-mile mark, according to the car's mileage, they came to the stone walls of a ruin on the right.

"Is this it?" Aaron didn't sound too sure.

"I don't know. There isn't anything else." Julie sounded even less positive.

He stopped the car on the road. There was no pull-off. "We might as well check it out. We've come this far."

They both got out of the car and approached the ruin.

"I wonder what it was," Julie said.

"Well," Aaron walked around the structure, only about one hundred feet square. "It's got four walls, but no entrance, no door in. That's odd." He peered over the five-foot high wall. "Nothing inside. Just overgrown vegetation."

Julie frowned. "I have to admit, I don't feel anything different yet. Maybe if we went inside it."

Aaron shook his head. "There's no easy way in. And it's too overgrown for us to try climbing the wall. I think this is another bust. That old guy just knew about this place and probably liked to get unsuspecting tourists to go out of their way. Probably his idea of a practical joke."

Julie tried a smile. "At least we can say we saw a vortex that few other people do."

"Yeah. Maybe." He picked up a small stone from the top of the wall. "But I'm taking something with me. There's nobody here to stop you from picking up a souvenir."

They got back in the car, and Aaron turned around to look behind him. "There's no place to turn around, but I don't want to back the whole way." He faced forward. "The road does keep going. There's got to be a place somewhere to turn around. A driveway or another road or something."

They drove ahead, following the arc of the road to the left, soon losing sight of the ruin behind them. The vegetation appeared to be getting both thicker and taller around them.

"You know, I haven't seen any houses or any kinds of buildings since we made that last turn." Julie broke the silence. "Or any kind of room to the side of the road."

Aaron agreed. "If it was two lanes, I could jockey my way around, but not on this narrow one-lane. If any other vehicles approach, we're in trouble. But I don't think that's going to happen. There's nothing out here to come from."

After another mile, he added, "This road keeps curving sharply to the left. I feel like I'm going in circles. I could have sworn we'd passed that particular tree with the knothole before. Wait just a minute." He stopped the car, but left the engine running and the door open as he stepped out. "I'll be right back."

"Wait! Where are you going? Don't leave me!" Julie reached for him, but too late.

He just waved his hand back at her and continued to the tree he had spotted. He pulled out the pen the old man had given him, stepped up to the tree, and scratched out a big cross with the tip of the pen just above the knothole, hoping it was deep enough to be visible from the road.

As he got back in the car, he checked that he could see it, and said, "I wasn't going to say anything, but I think we've passed that tree at least twice."

Julie put a hand to her mouth, but didn't speak.

"If that's so, then we are driving in circles and we should have come to the road we came in on." He turned to face her. "But I haven't seen any sign of a road. Or a lane or a path or any opening."

"Oh, my God." Her hand stayed at her mouth. "Are we, are we in the real vortex? Isn't that what a vortex is, a circle that keeps going around and around, around and around?"

He pulled out his phone and saw No Reception. "I don't know where we are." Aaron was looking straight ahead again. "We're going to drive some more and see if that damn tree shows up again."

After another ten minutes, with both of them straining to see any break in the vegetation, they both said, "Shit!" at the same time.

There was the tree and the cross.

Aaron kept going. "There's got to be a way out of here somewhere."

It wasn't until they passed it again that Julie spoke for the first time in a long while and in a small voice.

"Now what do we do?" Aaron could barely hear her. "What do we do? What do we do?"

He pulled up between a clump of cacti on the left and a big rock on the right, and stopped the engine. "Last time we went by here, I thought I saw a flash of something to the right. I'm going to go take a look."

"No! Don't you dare!" This time she did grab his arm and held on tightly. "Don't you go out there!"

He put his hand on hers and gently removed it from his arm. "Julie, we have to do something. I don't want to, but this is the only thing we have to go on. Otherwise, I keep driving until we run out of gas and then there will be no way back. Something flashed over there and I need to check it out. I'll only go in a few yards and, if I don't see anything, I'll come right back out. Here." He handed her the car keys. "Take these and keep the doors locked. If I'm not back in ten minutes, honk the car horn. And every five minutes after that. But I'll be back soon. I promise."

He leaned over to kiss her gently, then slid out the driver's door, pressing the lock button and closing it behind him. She pressed her hand to the window and watched him step around the rock and disappear into the darkness behind it.

######

Aaron took three steps into the plants, roughly pushing aside the branches and leaves, as there was no clear way through. He turned to orient himself to the car and stood in shock. He could not see the car or Julie.

He tried to force his way back where he had come from, but had gone well beyond the three steps before he stopped again. He should have been back to the road, or at least the rock, but they weren't where they were supposed to be.

He turned to the right and took a couple of steps, then back to the left for a few more. Still nothing. He took a deep breath. Doing this was just going to get him even more lost.

"Julie!" he yelled. "Julie, honk the horn." *Damn, I told her to keep the windows up. Wait a minute.* He stood silently, listening as hard as he could. *I can't hear anything. No birds, no wind, no critters in the underbrush. Nothing.*

Off to the right, there was a flash of movement.

I think that's what I saw before. There's something over there. He started in that direction, but paused, remembering he needed to listen for the car horn. The movement came again, and he pushed on toward it, rationalizing that it didn't seem too far and he should still be able to hear the horn.

After a couple of minutes of hacking his way through the underbrush, he suddenly came to a clearing, about twenty feet across in a perfect circle.

Sitting on a stone on the far side was the old man from the restaurant. Standing up and smiling, he came toward Aaron with his arms outstretched.

"You came! Thank God you came. I was hoping you would be the ones. I've been waiting for you."

He grabbed Aaron in a bear hug before the startled young man could react.

"What? What is this? What are you doing here?"

"I was waiting for somebody to come. I've been here a long time."

"What do you mean 'here'? You were at the restaurant this morning. And, even before you answer that, how do we get out of here? I'm totally lost. And my wife is back there in the car, lost too."

"Did you pick up a stone at the ruin?"

"Yes, but how did you ...?"

"Hold it in your hand."

Aaron dug into his pocket and brought out the stone. He held it in his right hand. At that instant, he heard the car horn. In the opposite direction from which he had come.

The older man took him by the arm. "There's an easier path in this direction. Keep holding onto that stone."

After five minutes, they heard another horn, then burst out of the undergrowth right in front of the car.

The passenger door flew open and Julie jumped out, running up to Aaron and throwing herself into his arms.

"You're back! Oh, thank God. I've been so worried. Where have you been? And how did you find him here?"

Aaron was reluctant to let her go, but eventually did. "I don't know where I was. But after a few scary minutes, I found him in a clearing, then we followed your car horn back."

"I've been honking it for an hour."

"I wasn't gone that long – maybe fifteen minutes."

"It's been an hour." She punched him in the chest. "But I was going to wait for you. You had promised to come back."

"And I did."

"And you did. But now what? We still can't get out of here."

The older man interrupted. "I can get you back to the main road. The first road out is just up here to the right."

Aaron and Julie looked at each other and slowly walked back to the car to get in. The older man got in the back seat. Aaron turned around to look at him.

"You can get us out of here. Really."

"Yes." The man nodded. "You have done what you needed to do. I've been waiting for a bridge to bring me back. It is time to return."

Aaron started the car and eased forward. Julie stayed facing the back seat.

"Who are you?"

"You'll see the turn coming up right about ... now."

Aaron spotted the opening that didn't exist before and Julie turned to exclaim, "That wasn't there before."

"You didn't need it before."

"The hell I didn't!" Aaron erupted.

"You're now back on Gulley Creek."

Aaron was still angry. "I don't remember ever getting off of Gulley Creek Drive."

Julie was facing the back seat again. "Now, once more, who are you?"

"My name is Owen Wolfe. Beyond that, there isn't anything else to explain. I'm just an ordinary guy that was lost. And now you found me."

Julie gasped. "Owen Wolfe? With an 'e' at the end?"

He nodded. "You'll be coming back up on Grainy Creek Road soon."

"But we haven't passed those stone ruins," Aaron pointed out.

"Probably not. You're going the other direction and you don't need them now, so they're probably not there anymore."

They reached the end of the road and saw the rock that said Gulley, or Galley, or Golley Creek, but nothing to indicate Grainy Creek.

"Turn left here." They turned left and drove silently until they found the fork with Grey Creek Drive. At that point, they turned right.

Wolfe spoke again. "I promised you a different kind of energy. I think you'll have to agree you won't forget this experience."

As they reached the main highway, he said, "You can let me out here."

Aaron frowned. "But there's nothing here."

"This is as far as I go. I can find my way from here."

Wolfe opened the door and stepped out. "I can't tell you how much it has meant to me for you to have come and found me. I hope you genuinely enjoy the rest of your trip and the rest of your lives."

Aaron found a gap in the traffic and pulled out. He desperately needed to get back to civilization, and, for the first time, actually appreciated seeing traffic.

Julie watched the figure of the old man as he got smaller in the distance. She checked her phone to find she now got reception, but didn't touch any buttons.

"I didn't tell you that when I looked up this vortex before, it spelled Wolf with an 'e' on the end. The Lost Wolfe Vortex. I thought it was just a variant spelling or something. But apparently not."

Aaron didn't respond for a moment, then spoke quietly. "I don't think I want to know anything more. But I know I am done with these vortices."

Old Man Sitting...

Old man sitting
On the front porch swing.
Come here, my son,
Let me tell you everything.

There's so much to life,
So much joy, so much pain.
We can't wait till it's past,
But we'd do it again.

We do what we must,
We do what we can.
We do what's been done
Till we make a new plan.

One song following
Another song soon.
We don't know the words
But we all hum the tune.

Old man sitting
On the front porch steps
Come here, my boy,
You're all I have left.

If ... you needed help immediately from someone or something, and, out of the blue, there were 'someones' to provide that assistance, what would you be expected to do in return? What would you be willing to pay forward?

GUARDIAN ANGELS

Teddy Lansing finished buttoning his overcoat, and stepped out into the snowy winter waiting for him outside his New York brownstone. He lifted a foot clad in his professional patent leather shoe, and sighed. Maybe he really should have put on the boots and carried the shoes, but his weather app had not been very accurate in telling him just how bad it was in the real world. He glanced around. There were only a couple of people moving very gingerly on the sidewalk, and burrowed so deeply in their winter garb that he had no idea who they were.

Eight steps led down his front stoop. Holding on to the railing, he took the first step. No problem. Slowly, another step. It was firm, no slipping. He switched the briefcase to his other hand, gripped the top of his coat tighter with the now free one, and confidently strode further down.

This time, he found the ice. His foot went out from under him. The other foot went up high, trying to recreate a balance that was no longer possible. He dropped the briefcase and grabbed for the railing, but his hands simply slid off the slick surface. His mind was working faster than his body, but not fast enough. *If I can hit with my rear first, maybe that will stop me.* He felt it land, but it didn't stop the sliding. *Maybe my back and elbows.* The middle of his back hit, but he could not get his elbows back in time. His head caught a step, and he stopped trying to prevent the problem, just hoping to survive it. His body carried him all the way to the foot of the steps, his head hitting all the rest of them.

He was vaguely aware of somebody coming up to him. "Are you alright? That looked bad. Can you move? Let me help you up."

Teddy didn't know what to say. He needed a minute to figure out just how he was.

Another voice called out. "No, don't move him." Good, he didn't really feel like moving. "We don't know how badly he is hurt." No, he didn't know either, and he wasn't quite ready to find out.

Another person covered him with a blanket. He hadn't realized that he had started shivering and now couldn't stop. Wondering about where the blanket had come from so quickly barely registered in his thoughts. Actually, thoughts were barely registering at all. Someone else seemed to be guiding passersby around him, and he briefly questioned where these helpers had all suddenly appeared from.

An older woman's face loomed over him. "Can you look at me?" His eyes tried to focus on her features. "Good, don't try to move your head right now. Help is on the way. Can you wiggle your toes?"

Teddy tried. He shrugged with his facial muscles and attempted to speak. "I don't know. I think so, but it's so cold, I can't tell." It had been so hard to say anything that he wasn't sure if it had actually been audible or merely thinking it to himself. But the woman nodded and said, "Okay. We'll wait for the experts."

He did feel somebody adjusting the blanket, which was probably a good thing that he was aware of that sensation. At least he thought he felt it. He blinked his eyes and tried to push his hands against the ground, but couldn't tell if anything was working. He knew he didn't rise at all, and stopped trying. In the distance, he could hear sirens and hoped they were for him.

He wanted to tell himself that this was all silly, that he had just fallen, to give him a minute, and he would get up and dust himself off. But he didn't really feel like that. It was better to just lie here and wait. He focused again on the woman's face and she smiled and brushed hair away from his forehead. That's better, he thought. We can wait. He closed his eyes, but just for a moment.

######

Teddy found himself slouching in the back seat of a car, behind the driver. He pulled himself up straight and moved his left hand to find his seatbelt fastened. Realizing that he had moved his hand, he held it up in front of him, rotating it, then held up the other arm. "I'm alright. I'm not hurting."

He must have said it out loud, because a feminine voice next to him said, "Hi, glad to see you're with us now. You had us worried for a minute. Or two."

He turned to find a young woman on the seat to the right of him. Not the same woman who had been reassuring him before, but this one smiled at him, too. Which reassured him, but only slightly.

"You are fine. Maybe a little confused, but everybody is at first. And you'll be back home before you know it. At least that's what they tell me."

"Where, where am I?"

"In the back seat of a car right now. But you probably already guessed that. We're on our way to rescue somebody else."

"Rescue? What do you mean?"

"That's what we're supposed to do." She shrugged. "And, I guess, now you are too. It's your turn."

"I, I ..." He looked out the window. There was no snow and they appeared to be on a mountain road. He touched the glass. It wasn't cold. "I was lying on the ground. In the snow. I had slipped on the icy steps and I couldn't get up."

She nodded. "I know. We saved you. So now it's your turn to help someone else."

He shook his head, confused, then was mildly surprised there was no pain. "There was this older woman who was talking to me, calming me down."

"That was Martha. You were her fourth case. Or do I mean client? Patient? Rescuee? I don't know what the right word would be. So, she should now be back in the hospital, recovering from the heart attack that started her. You were my first one."

"Fourth? First? What are you talking about? Who are you?"

"Oh." She looked out the front window, then back at him and stuck out her hand. "It looks like we have some time yet. I am Megan. I fell out of a boat. And never learned how to swim. Tom," she pointed to the older man in the passenger seat in front of her, "was being mugged by a gang. A loose wire shocked the driver, Teller, in his apartment.

"The point is that we were all going to die until we were saved. By those that came before us." She sighed. "Just like you were. You had some damage to your neck and spine, and may have died if somebody had moved you or not called for an ambulance quick enough. If we hadn't been there. And now, each of us has a debt to pay by saving four other lives, before we can return to our own life. At least that's what Tom told me just before your fall."

There was a loud screech of tires and a tremendous crash from the road in front of them. A weaving pickup truck roared by them, picking up speed. But ahead of them, a car, which seemed to have been forced off the road, had crashed into a large boulder.

Megan turned around to watch the receding truck. "Okay, I got the license number, D45JT." She faced Teddy. "Now, you begin."

Teller pulled the car in behind the accident. Both he and Tom immediately jumped out. Teddy put his hand on the door handle, but hesitated and looked at Megan.

"Go," she waved him on. "This may take more muscle than I have. I'm calling 911."

Teddy opened the door and sprinted to the wrecked car. Tom, being more elderly than Teddy had at first realized, was in the street, ready to wave traffic around. Teller was at the driver's door. Teddy opened the passenger door and saw that there was only the driver in the vehicle, but that the seatbelt needed unfastened to get the occupant out. He reached through a pile of papers on the seat and undid the belt, then hurried around the car to help Teller lift the driver out. They carried him back toward their car and laid him on the ground, just before a flame started in the front seat of the crashed vehicle.

Both he and Teller were panting from their efforts. Teller gasped, "Whoa, I guess that's why we were needed. I didn't see a fire coming."

Teddy leaned back against the front of their car. "I saw a packet of cigarettes among the papers that flew everywhere. He must have been a smoker, and there was possibly a lit one somewhere in that mess."

Tom was now talking with the driver of a sedan that had stopped. The driver pulled over across the road, then hurried to their side. "I'm a doctor. I can take a look at him."

Megan joined them. "An ambulance, a fire truck, and police are on their way. Plus, they're on a lookout for the driver of that pickup."

Tom came up to them. As they heard the sirens, Teller wiped his hands together and said, "I think I may be done ..."

Teddy realized they were walking down a neighborhood street with sidewalks, and trees shading the front porches from the bright afternoon sun. They weren't hurrying, but Tom and Megan, in front, were setting a steady pace.

"What the ...? Where am I?" The man beside him suddenly stopped and cringed away from them. "What's going on?"

Teddy saw the others were halted a few feet away, and realized that it was his turn to explain.

"I'm Teddy. That's Megan and Tom."

"Whe-where's my car? I was in my car." He was looking around him in confusion. Teddy noted that the two others were swiveling their heads, but seemingly with a purpose. "There was a pickup coming right at me. I couldn't stay on the road."

"You were in an accident. Your car hit a boulder. But you're alright now. We got you out. We, I guess we rescued you."

"I, I don't remember."

Teddy shrugged. "Probably not. You were unconscious when we pulled you from the car. An ambulance and fire truck were on the way. The way I understand it is that we saved you, and now you need to be part of saving someone else. Actually, I think you have to save four other people. That's what they told me. You're my first, so I have three more to go."

"What are you talking about? I'm okay. I feel okay." The man shook his head.

Teddy sighed. "I know. I felt the same way. I slipped on an icy step and cracked my head. Probably fractured my skull. They, and two others, saved me. Megan was, um, drowning, I think it was, and Tom was being mugged. I don't know what part of us is really here, but we were all rescued, and now, so I was told, we have to rescue others."

"I'm supposed to be part of rescuing someone?"

Teddy put out his hand and touched the other man's shoulder. "I wish there was a manual I could just give you. Apparently, we just have to do it."

"Smoke! I see smoke from that back window." Megan pointed to a house around the next corner. "Let's go. That has to be for us." Tom headed for the front door, with Teddy close behind him. The smoke was becoming stronger.

"Fire?" the man cried. "I don't know anything about fires."

"Good," said Megan. "Then you can call 911."

He pulled out his phone. "Where are we?"

She pointed to the corner street sign and glanced at the house. "I think we are at 111 Hemmenthaler," and hurried after the others.

"Hemmen..., what?"

"Just call!" she yelled over her shoulder.

As she came up to the house, Tom was tentatively putting out a hand for the doorknob. "No one is answering the bell or a knock." He grasped the knob and slowly opened the door.

"Aren't we supposed to wait for the firemen?" Teddy asked. "They don't want just anybody entering a burning building. We don't have any smoke masks or anything."

Tom stepped over the threshold. "If we had time to wait, I don't think we'd be here." He indicated the three of them. "You two head that way and I'll go into this back room."

Teddy and Megan hurried down a hallway to the room where the smoke had been coming from. Through the open doorway, a haze was developing.

Along the far wall, a woman was asleep on a bed with a book fallen open across her chest. There was the start of a small flame among the papers on a desk behind her head, and sparks were still jumping from a lamp.

Teddy grabbed a spare blanket and threw it over the desk, then reached down and quickly yanked the lamp cord out of the wall. Megan gently shook the woman, and she woke up, startled.

"Wha-what? Who are you?"

"There's a fire in your house. We need to get you out, now." Megan helped her sit up.

The woman noticed the smoke, and Teddy still patting at the blanket. "Oh! Oh, I just lay down to read for a little bit. The baby! Lilly, in the next room! She was napping!"

"Megan, you go get the baby." Teddy reached for the woman. "I'll get her out." He helped the woman to her feet. "We've called for the firetruck. It's on its way."

"And the dog!" the woman cried.

He heard a whimpering from the front door. "I think somebody already has the dog." With Megan carrying the baby in front of him, Teddy guided the woman through the door and onto the front lawn. The new guy was there, still holding the phone, standing next to Tom, holding the dog by a leash.

The new guy said, "The firefighters are coming." Then asked, "Is there anybody else?"

The young woman coughed, then took the baby from Megan and shook her head. "No, no. My husband is at work. I had to get up a few times during the night with Lilly, and I guess I just fell asleep. Do you know how the fire started?"

Teddy responded, "It looks like sparks were coming from the cord on the lamp."

"That old lamp? We got that from his aunt. A family heirloom. We just hadn't gotten around to replacing it yet."

A fire truck pulled up in front of the house, just as a neighbor came running over. Tom handed the dog to the neighbor, and they all took a step back, letting the experts take over....

######

The four of them were now sitting in what appeared to be a waiting room. The room was full of young women, and it took Teddy a moment to realize they were all in different stages of pregnancy. A doctor's office. A waiting room in a doctor's office.

He looked at the others. Tom was gone. It was now himself, Megan, the new guy, and the young woman. The woman was staring at them.

"You were at my house. We were on my front lawn." Her voice was rising. "Where did you take me? Where is Lilly?"

The new guy was sitting next to her. He looked at Teddy with his eyes raised. Teddy merely shrugged and pointed at him. "Your turn."

The man turned back and put his hand on the young woman's hand. "It's okay, Lilly is fine. My name is Tony. We're all here to rescue someone else."

The woman's eyes opened wide. "What do you mean?"

As Tony sighed and began to explain what he had been told, Teddy poked Megan and whispered, "What do you think we're here for? I know nothing about babies."

Megan kept looking around the room. "I don't know, but something is going to happen here, and it's going to take us responding. Immediately. We have to keep our eyes open."

Teddy started looking around, too, for anything that might appear to be out of the ordinary, but not enough to get everybody else's attention. Out of the corner of his mouth, he asked, "Have you noticed something? All of the men's names have started with a 'T'. That seems kind of odd."

"You finally noticed that, huh? And all of the women start with 'M'." She leaned forward and interrupted Tony to ask the woman down several seats, "Excuse me, what's your name?"

"Uh, Meredith."

Megan sat back. "See, I told you. My best guess is that there are more, um, teams than just us doing this sort of work. And we're the 'T' and 'M' team. What that means, I don't know, but it can't be only 'T' and 'M' people getting saved. There must be a lot of other people rescuing other initials." She shrugged. "I'm sure there are always a bunch of people needing to be helped." She pointed at a woman grimacing and pushing herself up out of a chair. "We may be on."

The woman walked very slowly to the hallway, leaned against the wall for a moment, then tried the door of the Women's room. Megan got up to follow her around the corner, but the door appeared to be locked, and the woman moved even more slowly to the receptionist window.

"Excuse me." She was beginning to pant. "I really need to use a bathroom and there must be someone in this one."

The receptionist pointed to the door leading into the general hallway. "There is one right outside that door. It's probably closer than the staff one back here."

"Thank you." She pushed away from the counter and shook her head. Megan stepped up and offered her an arm.

"Here, I'm going that way. Let me help." They moved through the outer door, and Megan waved for Teddy to come behind her. He put his hand on Tony's shoulder, interrupting him again, then gestured for the two of them to follow him.

The expectant mother pushed the bathroom door open, and they heard a loud thump as the door swung closed behind her. Megan hurried through the door, and Teddy could see the woman's body lying on the floor.

Megan called behind her, "Meredith, go tell the receptionist that one of the women has fallen in the bathroom. Quickly! Now!"

Meredith ran off and Megan knelt beside the woman. Teddy and Tony moved into the room.

"Did she slip?"

Megan shook her head. "She just fell. She's unconscious. Here, come help me lay her on her back."

As they rolled her over, Tony knelt at her feet. "This is what I do. I'm an obstetrician. Teddy, I saw a blanket on one of the chairs out there. Grab it and we'll put it under her head." He rolled up his sleeves.

Teddy found the blanket and brought it back, handing it to Megan, who rolled it up and set it under the woman's head. The woman was moaning slightly.

"I don't think it's labor," Tony said. "It could be low blood sugar, or an issue with her blood pressure. Those are not that uncommon." He felt her wrist for the pulse.

Teddy moved back out into the hallway and held the door for Meredith, leading another woman wearing a white coat. Then Teddy and Meredith stepped back while the doctor and a nurse carrying a medical kit pushed past them.

"What's going on?" Meredith asked.

Teddy shrugged. "She just passed out. On the bathroom floor. Tony thinks it could be her blood sugar level or her blood pressure."

"What are we supposed to do?"

"I think we are here to get her through the initial crisis. If it wasn't for us, she may have lain on that floor for a while. No one else may have come out here. This, apparently, is what we do."

As two other medical personnel ran up, Megan and Tony came out through the door. Tony was rolling his sleeves back down. "I think they have it now. We just need to get out of their way."

Megan was smiling. "Thank you all for everything. This has been ...."

*****

Teddy was now in the driver's seat of a car, with Tony to his right. Meredith and the still pregnant mother were in the back seat. They were sitting in a parking lot, apparently waiting for something to occur.

Tony looked down. "My pants are clean. How did that happen? They were dirty from the floor a minute ago."

"Whatever you did seemed to have helped."

"She was really out of it. I think it was an issue with the blood pressure. Or low blood sugar. Those things can happen. More frequently than we'd like to imagine." He realized he was repeating what he had said earlier, and pointed a thumb at the backseat. "The other doctor and the nurse had it under control when we left."

In the back seat, Meredith was working at calming down the other woman, letting her know that she herself was recently a new mother. The woman was close to hysterical in not knowing what was going on with her baby, but did recognize the others as people trying to help her. Meredith told her who they were and asked her name. "Mischa." She then told her about their role now in helping others in need, and that included Mischa being a helper. She finished with, "I think, after you're done, you just go back to that moment and everyone will be fine. You'll see. You'll just have to see."

A pickup truck entered the parking lot in front of them, weaving first right, then left, seemingly out of control.

"Another accident?" Teddy asked.

They watched for a moment, trying to figure out just where they were going to have to be and when they were going to have to be there. Teddy started the car, to be ready to go.

He saw a group of teenagers come out of the store attached to the parking lot, totally oblivious to anything else around them. One of them pointed to a car further away, and they started walking toward it, talking and laughing. The truck, while still at the other end of the lot, began weaving in their general direction.

Teddy called out, "Get out of the car! Now! Run after me. It's going to happen over there!"

Tony and Meredith immediately jumped out. Mischa hesitated, then joined them outside the car. Teddy took off for what he hoped was an interception point between the pickup and the teenagers.

The kids' attentions were still on each other and their ride in front of them. The truck, though not in a straight line, was definitely heading in their direction. Teddy sped up, changing his angle slightly.

He crashed into the passenger side of the pickup, knocking it into another parked car, about forty feet away from the group. They stopped in shock, suddenly quiet, and stared at the accident.

Tony came running up to Teddy's door. "Are you alright?"

Teddy wasn't sure yet, but told him, "Yeah, I'm fine. Check on the driver."

Tony ran over to the truck, with Mischa following as fast as she could move. Teddy slowly backed away from it, giving them room. Mischa yelled to the kids, "Everybody okay?"

Meredith tugged open his front door and took his arm to help him out. "We already called for help. The police, at least, are on their way. Did you get hurt?", noticing that he winced as he put his left foot down.

"I think I banged my knee. But it's nothing compared to where I'm going to be in a few minutes." He pointed to the license plate on the pickup. "See that plate?"

"Yeah, D45JT, what about it?"

"You won't have known, but that's the same truck that first forced Tony off the road. When I saw that, I knew that, even if the rest of you were here to rescue that driver, I wasn't. I was here to save them." And he gestured to the teenagers.

Tony and Mischa had gotten the driver out and sat him against the side of his truck. Teddy noticed two of the kids pulling phones from their pockets.

"Any second now, they're going to start taking pictures. I don't think anyone is supposed to know who we are."

Meredith took off a shoe and threw it against the teenagers' car. They all turned to look at it, then swiveled back with their cameras ready.

But Teddy's car and the four strangers were gone ....

Teddy's eyes fluttered open. The unfamiliar woman leaning over him noticed and touched his arm. "You had a bad fall. You're in the back of an ambulance on the way to the hospital. I think you hit your head badly, but overall, your signs are stable." She smiled. "You're going to be alright. But don't try to move your body at all. We have your head immobilized, because we don't know how much damage there is to your skull. However, you're conscious and your blood pressure is good. Those are good signs."

He croaked out, barely audible. "What about the other people that were there? The ones protecting me?"

She shook her head. "I don't know about any other people. We were just focused on you. Maybe they're the ones who placed a blanket over you? And called us?"

The images of the other rescuers were merging in his head. "We went on..." He weakly coughed. "We went on and saved others. We had to save so many before we could come back. Four, I think it was." His voice faded.

"Good for you." She nodded, but more in acknowledgement than in agreement. "We need more people saving others. Too many people just walk the other way."

"I wonder if I'll ever see them again."

He spoke so quietly that she leaned in close to ask him, "Did you say something?"

He wanted to shake his head, as the comment hadn't been for her, but couldn't because of the brace. "That's okay."

She adjusted something and smiled again. "Good. You just lie there and take care of yourself."

Teddy attempted to smile back. He wasn't sure that the smile actually showed on his face, but, at the moment, he was okay with that.

If ... a rather incompetent and ill-prepared gang attempts a kidnapping, what are the odds that it will go well? Or go extremely badly?

WHERE DREAMS GO TO DIE

"Watch your step."

It was a starless night, and Cheryl led the way for her fellow kidnappers through the dark back patio with her flashlight. "Ernie drained the pool, but he wanted to let it dry before covering it up. He'll be back here in the morning."

Mitch grunted in exasperation and rolled his eyes, though nobody could see them. "We know, Cheryl. We came this way when we entered the house. Remember? For Christ' sake, we're not kids." He glanced back at Tiny pushing Old Man Randall's wheelchair. "Well, I'm not, anyway."

Too many football concussions had not shrunk Tiny's six-foot, six-inch frame, but had dulled his thinking. And his playing weight of three hundred and forty pounds was now just fat, without the muscle needed to carry it around. Even though it was the middle of the night, sweat was glistening off his forehead and his face grimaced in pain.

"Mitch, I gotta stop."

"Now what?" Mitch turned on him. "You been complaining all night. We were late getting in the house because you had to keep stopping. And we've been moving slow getting out. We have to go."

"Yeah, Tiny." Cheryl swung her flashlight back in their direction. "And I've got to get back in and lock myself in the closet, so the family don't know it was me who brought you into this. I told you not to eat your usual six hot dogs tonight. You're already too fat."

"It's not my stomach that's hurting. It's up here." Tiny tapped his chest and groaned. "Ah, it hurts."

Mitch dropped the bag he'd been carrying, full of miscellaneous golden trinkets, silver, and money from around the house, intended to initially confuse any kidnapping investigation into also looking at robbery. He walked over to Tiny and looked up from his own five-feet, four inches. "I don't care where it hurts. We've got to get out of here. Now move it." He poked him hard in the stomach for emphasis.

Old Man Randall, rich Old Man Randall, very rich and very Old Man Randall, and the subject of this kidnapping enterprise, was barely conscious, but enough to be annoyed at the bickering. He slightly turned his head toward Cheryl, vaguely aware that his night nurse was taking him somewhere. But he was past caring and only wanted to go back to bed.

Tiny stepped away from the back of the wheelchair and faced Mitch. He opened his mouth as if to say something, but quickly closed it with a surprised look on his face. His mouth fell open again, then he stopped breathing and fell straight forward on top of Mitch, completely enveloping him.

Cheryl darted over to them. One of Mitch's hands was visible, but was ineffectively tapping at the concrete poolside. Muffled sounds were coming from under Tiny's body. She poked at Tiny.

"Get up, you stupid ... get up. You're smothering him."

Tiny didn't move. His eyes were open, but staring at nothing but the past. Cheryl tried pushing his body, but the weight was too much for her. She frantically looked around for something to use to pry him, but all the patio furniture had been put away for the winter. Her light fell on the net that was used to clean debris out of the pool. She grabbed it, and ran back, trying to fit it under Tiny to leverage him off Mitch. But she still couldn't get his body to move.

The sounds were becoming fainter, and the hand had stopped moving. She dropped the net and backed away. She shone her light on Old Man Randall. His eyes were open, but he couldn't help, even if he knew what was going on.

She took a couple of steps in the direction of the get-away van, parked on the other side of the gate, then turned and took two steps toward the inside of the house. To leave or to follow through with her part of the plan, to lock herself in the closet and pretend that she had been an innocent victim the whole time? Her mind wouldn't function, and she moved back and forth several times, becoming more and more frantic.

She threw up her hands, aiming the light at the sky, and just ran. Her feet hit the bag of stolen loot and she went flying forward. The flashlight tumbled out of her hand and down the twelve feet into the bottom of the empty pool, shattering itself and lying forever more useless. A brief second later, Cheryl joined it. At both the bottom of the pool and the forever uselessness.

Old Man Randall's eyes flicked towards the pool, then back to Tiny's body lying in front of him. The noises from underneath had stopped. He chuckled, almost audibly, then sighed and leaned back, his breathing slowing until it too stopped.

In the morning, Ernie was surprised to see an unfamiliar van sitting next to the gate, but it was nothing compared to his reaction when he saw what was waiting beside the pool.

If ... your high school reunion committee was having trouble agreeing on certain aspects of the celebration, would there be a way to resolve those problems? To ensure that everybody was happy by the time of the reunion? Maybe not....

50TH REUNION: DO OR DIE

Dark clouds were rolling in, but no rain had yet started as George and Susan Peabody entered Mac's Café. Finally, the night of their fiftieth high school reunion had arrived, but Susan was still nervous. Supposedly a joyous occasion, all she could think of was the last nine months of constant drama for the reunion committee, before they could give birth to the actual event.

When she had originally volunteered to be on the eight-member committee, it had seemed like a good idea. The class had only been ninety-two strong to begin with, and just fifty-five were either still surviving or could be found, so Mac's Café was an easy choice for the site. She expected little beyond a meal and maybe a cake. After all, it was just an opportunity for people to see each other, ones that had maintained their friendships, and ones that hadn't been seen in those fifty years.

But, as it turned out, it was difficult to agree on anything.

"George, I hope this goes well tonight. I'm just afraid something is going to go wrong."

"That's the fourth time you've said that tonight, Susan. So far." He held the door for her.

"Yes, but there were so many ugly petty disagreements. A buffet versus a served dinner, a disc jockey spinning records versus a band, whether to have flowers at all the tables, the flavor of cake, who to have as a photographer, corsages for the women, the fancifulness of the nametags, whether or not to have presentations, whether they should be serious or funny. Anything and everything took weeks of discussion and there was always at least one 'Well, I don't know,' to gum up whatever had already been decided."

"Well, we are here now. Whatever is going to happen is going to happen. We'll get through the evening. There is going to be a dinner, and music, and, maybe, if you're lucky, some dancing."

Marcia Terry was sitting at the front table, signing guests in and handing out nametags. The tags were outlined with school colors, and the names were carefully stylized, but they did not contain the little colored dots indicating the school activities that had been participated in by the alumnus. These had been a main point of contention, particularly from those involved in a lot of activities. They still wanted to show off a little, with those dots like medals to display proudly on their chests. However, it had been decided that those with no dots might become a little embarrassed. And there was also the issue of just plain forgetting that someone had been in something, like the choir or the senior play. It was enough that they had been omitted being listed in those activities in the yearbook in the first place.

"Hi, Marcia." Marcia stood up and Susan gave her a hug. "How many have we had come in so far?"

"Oh, about half. I think that's about the way it is with these types of things. So many want to arrive early, and so many were never on time for anything. A lot of them are looking first at the Memorial Wall." The listing of the deceased classmates displayed next to the door. "Apparently, they want to know who not to look for. It was sad to add John Adkins and Sandy Stillwater so recently. Since they were members of the reunion committee, they're at the top of the list with a special dedication for them."

"Yes, I know." Susan patted her shoulder. "I don't think John's heart attack was too surprising to people that knew him. He hadn't been well for a while. But Sandy being killed in that hit and run just last week ...." She shook her head.

Marcia turned to Susan's husband. "George, do you know if anything is going on with that investigation?"

George shook his head. "If there is, they haven't told me." He had finally retired after a long career in the police department, but still frequently checked in at the station, and filled in when a body was needed for something routine.

He noticed a line was starting to form behind them, but Susan had one more question for Marcia, this time in a whisper. "I hate to ask this, but have you seen Gloria Hramosky yet?"

Marcia paused, before responding in her normal voice. "No, but I'm certain we'll know when she does arrive. There will be something to complain about, I'm sure. For some reason or another, she wasn't happy about any of the final decisions."

George took Susan by the arm. "I think it's time for us to find where we're supposed to sit."

Marcia called after them. "Jack's already at the committee table. He insisted on driving me over early." Jack was her dutiful husband, who always had her best interests at heart.

Carl and Becky Wolscheimer, the only other still-married classmates, asked them to join their table, but Susan had to shake her head. "I'd much rather sit with you, but I think there's supposed to be a reunion committee table, and we better at least set a drink down there." She sighed. "Gloria insisted we have our own table. As if we haven't spent enough time together."

There had originally been five couples married from the class, but two had divorced and one was now widowed, leaving only the Peabodys and the Wolscheimers.

They found their table, the biggest one of all, and right in the center of the room. There had initially been thirteen ("a lucky 13," thought Susan) seats at the table, but they were now down by three. Two chairs were shrouded in black crepe paper for the recent deaths, and John's widow, who had not been in the class, did not want to attend by herself. Sandy, not with anyone at the time of her death, had twice been widowed. That left three married couples, Joe Settler bringing a date, Pete Hampshire, a widower, and Gloria, who had never married. Pete and Marcia's husband, Jack, were already at the table, as well as the final couple, Lewis and Betty Atwell.

Susan had to admit to herself that John Adkins' death had alleviated some tension, as he and Lewis, who had been best friends since fifth grade, had almost come to blows disagreeing about the style of special awards to be presented later. John had wanted some silly, somewhat insulting ones, like most marriages or most weight change, but Lewis had wanted to stick with nicer ones, such as who traveled the furthest or who had lived in the most states. By default, Lewis was now in charge of presentations. "The Most Recent Death" had been one of John's suggestions, but would not be awarded now.

"Come to think of it," she whispered to George, who had not been aware that she had been thinking of anything at all, "Sandy's death also made choosing the type of cake easier. She had wanted a tiered cake. Like for a wedding, but with the king and queen of the prom on top."

"Wasn't she the Prom Queen?" George whispered back.

"Yes," said Susan. "And Steve McKernick, the Prom King, isn't even going to be here. Something about being otherwise engaged. So, Sandy would have had the glory all to herself."

Pete overheard them and asked, "Wasn't Steve dating Marcia at that time? Before she met Jack, of course," as he saw Jack watching them.

"Yes, I think you may be right." Susan decided to quickly change the subject, because Sandy dancing so much with Steve that night had been a sore subject for Marcia for a long time. "Jack, Marcia said you came very early tonight."

"Yeah, she wanted me to drive her over so that we wouldn't have both cars here. She didn't want the parking lot to be too crowded, especially with the storm coming later. And you know her. We were two hours early, just so she could make sure everything was just right. And, in case Gloria also got here early and had changed some things. She wouldn't have put it past Gloria to have moved some tables or added some decorations of her own." He shook his head. "Having worked in advertising, she wanted to glitz everything up."

At that moment, Joe Settler arrived at the table, brushing rain out of his hair, and towing a slightly younger man along with him. "Hi, everybody, just for your information, the rain has started. And I'd like you all to meet

Freddie March," indicating the newcomer. "Freddie, everybody will let you know who they are."

There were at least two "Oh"s, and, to be even, a couple of "Ah"s. Only George said, "Nice to meet you, Freddie. I'm George Peabody, and my wife Susan."

Betty Atwell asked, "Do you still go by 'Freddie'? At our age?"

He laughed. "Only Joe calls me that. To everyone else, I'm 'Fred'. But then I sometimes call him 'Joey'." He winked. "But not tonight."

"Glad you could be with us, Fred," Jack, who was called 'Jackie' only during certain intimate moments, said. "I'm Jack Terry. Take a seat." The others gave their names, but Fred merely nodded, knowing it was going to take some practice to recall all of them.

Joe sat and looked around the table. "Is Gloria off readjusting somewhere? Or just plain criticizing? She's not happy if she's not complaining about something or other."

"No." Susan's head swiveled to view the room. "No one has seen her yet. It is odd that she wouldn't have been here by now."

Jack raised a glass. "Well, let us appreciate the moment, then. To the continued harmony of this table throughout the evening."

They all took a sip of whatever they were drinking and resumed asking questions of Fred. George set down his glass of orange juice and ginger ale, and stood. "Susan, I'm going to get something to snack on while we're waiting for the buffet to open. Do you want anything?"

"No, since we now have someone new at the table, I'm going to stay here and see what I can learn."

George filled up at the appetizer table, then wandered over to the entrance door, chewing as he talked. "Sam, I didn't know you were going to be here."

"Hey, George." Sam Getty was a member of the Summerfield Police Department and was trying, unsuccessfully, to look inconspicuous, as he was probably forty years younger than anybody else. "I'm doing security tonight. Apparently, none of this group is considered trustworthy. Especially that table there in the middle. They all look guilty of something to me."

George nodded. "I can understand that. I haven't trusted any of them for years. Let me know if you need any help when you catch one of them pocketing the silverware."

Sam chuckled, "I will."

George nodded at Marcia checking in another couple. He noticed that Gloria Hramosky's nametag was still sitting on the table. He muttered, "Curious, curious," and moved off.

He joined Susan, who had now gone over to talk with the Wolscheimers. "George, did you know that Carl and Becky are going on a cruise around Italy this fall?"

George, who had never been the slightest bit interested in the Wolscheimer's vacation plans, merely shook his head.

Carl said, "Gloria went on this trip last year and told us all about it. She said that she was going to do something Italian for tonight, sort of as a surprise for everybody. That no one else knew anything about it." He looked at all the decorations. "I don't see anything Italian."

Susan put her hand to her mouth. "Oh, no. She did want to do mock-up pictures of the committee in the style of Michelangelo to put up on the ceiling."

"Weren't those a lot of nudes?" Becky asked.

Susan ruefully nodded. George took her arm. "Would you excuse us for a minute?"

They walked a few steps away. George panned the room. "Now, maybe she changed the menu to all pizzas, or she is going to make a grand entrance covered in spaghetti sauce.... But I suspect it's more likely that she has already been here. It's not like Gloria to wait till the last minute."

"What do you mean, George?"

"I'm going to get Sam and we're going to take a look throughout the entire restaurant. It's not very big. It shouldn't take long."

"What are you looking for?"

George sighed. "I don't know yet. I hope nothing."

He reluctantly set his plate down at an empty table, and waved for Sam to come join him at the entrance to the kitchen area. "Big Mac" MacIntire, the owner of the café, was supervising the setting up of the buffet. It smelled delicious, but George had to look past the food right now.

"Mac, I hate to disturb you."

"What do you need, George?" Mac had played professional football and believed in getting to the point.

"We are missing somebody that should have been here a long time ago. I wonder if Sam and I can take a look around the rest of the building."

"You talking about Gloria Hramosky? Tina said she saw her come in earlier, but I don't think anybody's seen her since."

"Has anyone been in the back room?"

"Nope, haven't needed it tonight. We could fit your entire class in this front area. And we're closed to the public for this event." He waved to the buffet. "Marge, Tina, and Tommy can handle this. Come on."

Mac walked them through the kitchen and opened the inner door leading to their overflow area. He switched on the lights and they looked around. Tables and chairs were set up as in the front area, but without tablecloths or place settings. They could see the rain splashing against the windows facing the street. Several large square packages were leaning against the back wall.

George pointed. "What are those, Mac?"

Mac frowned. "I don't know. They weren't there earlier today."

Sam hurried over to them. "They sort of look like big picture frames, all wrapped up." He pulled one back up to find several more behind it, then straightened those up, and gasped. "George, I think you better look at this."

George looked and took a deep breath. "Yeah." It took another moment for him to continue. "That's the missing Gloria Hramosky."

Mac lifted the rest of the frames packages away to clear them of the body. Sam knelt down and made a show of taking her pulse, but her open eyes hadn't seen anything for some time. "Looks like somebody has strangled her."

"Sam, you better call it in. Mac, don't let anyone back here."

Mac tried the outside door, but found it still locked, then went to tell Marge to keep the kitchen staff out of the room. Sam got off his radio and shrugged.

"I got in touch with Marie, at dispatch. Seth is on call tonight, but he got called out to an accident caused by the storm. The others are unavailable, and the newbie, Carly Duncan, is babysitting her newborn. Marie told me Carly can call her husband to get him home from his volleyball night, and Seth will get over when he can, but it may be a while for either of them. Forensics and Dr. Ross, the coroner, are on their way over."

George walked back to the kitchen door and stood there for a moment. "Crap. I believe we have a room full of suspects, and it's up to you and I, Sam, to try to figure out what happened before this storm clears, and people start heading home." He came back to the framed packages. "But first, let's see what we have here."

One package had already been opened, but the wrapping had been draped back over the picture. He pulled the paper away and held up the frame. "Oh, my."

George wasn't familiar with the particular art or artist, but it had a Renaissance feel to it. It depicted three nude figures – a muscular male, probably one of the Roman gods, grasping a voluptuous maiden in his arms, smiling up at him, but with another female holding on to his leg as if to keep him from leaving. Pasted onto the passionate couple were the senior yearbook faces of Sandy Stillwater and Steve McKernick, with Marcia Terry's face on the nubile young woman being abandoned.

Sam didn't recognize the features. "Those are some bodies, but who are the faces?"

George shook his head and set it down. "It was intended to embarrass someone in particular. Actually, to humiliate that person." He picked up another one and pulled the paper back. It depicted another couple from the committee in all their glory, but at least they were a couple. A third one showed two naked men embracing. One was Joe and the other face was of a male, not on the committee, but currently married and currently present with his wife. None of the faces were recognizable to Sam, as they were all from fifty years ago, but most of the attendees at the dinner would have known them.

Slowly, he opened a fourth one. "Okay, I could take this one home." George had never liked his yearbook picture, but Susan's more than made up for it, and it was only the two of them. Sam tried to step around to see it, but George turned it to face the wall. "Not for your eyes. For the moment, I'm going to leave the rest of them still wrapped up." He turned all of them to face the wall, but set away from his.

"I think we have our immediate motive. These would have been extremely embarrassing for the entire committee, but particularly this first one. The one that had been opened. I think Gloria may have enjoyed showing that one. Privately at first, so that she could see the expression on someone's face. She just wouldn't have enjoyed that expression for very long."

George walked to the kitchen door. "Sam, I would suggest you stay here with the body. Let the lab people in through this door." He gestured to the door from the outside. "Don't let anyone see that separate piece of art. Please."

"I won't. I promise." Sam shook his head.

"I'm going back to the table and see what's what. We won't disrupt the reunion. Yet."

Mac was waiting for him next to the door leading to the front room. He raised an eyebrow in unspoken question.

"Mac, we're not going to announce anything at this point. Not till the other police officers get here, anyway."

"I got you. We started serving the buffet. The food was ready, and I didn't know how long you'd be."

"Good. No need to waste it. If someone could get a plate to Sam, I'm sure he'd appreciate it. Gloria won't be eating her portion."

George nodded to the people in line at the buffet and walked slowly back to his table. Marcia had joined the group, and George glanced at the table next to the entrance. Only one nametag appeared to still be there.

Everyone had a plate in front of them. Susan looked at him, but didn't say anything. Marcia was talking and waving a wineglass.

"Hey, George. Wondered where you went to. Everybody's here except for Gloria. But I think she can find her own name at the table." She laughed. "I left it right in the middle so she wouldn't miss it. She's probably got something planned as a grand entrance, but let's enjoy the dinner until she gets here." She took what was much more than a sip from her glass.

Jack raised his drink. "Yes, to the evening for as long as we can."

George took his seat, but didn't join the others in a drink.

"George?" Susan looked questioningly at him. He raised his right hand slightly, as if to indicate not now, then put it back down.

"Marcia, I understand Jack drove you here quite early tonight."

She took another gulp. "Oh, yes, I had a lot of last-minute things to get done. Setting up the table, arranging the names, finishing the Memorial Board. I always panic at the last minute. It was nice of him to offer to bring me."

"Jack, what were you doing during that time?"

Marcia answered for him. "Oh, he had some book with him. I think it was a crossword puzzle book, something like that. He can keep himself busy, can't you, Jack? In fact, I didn't even see him most of the time."

She waved her glass high. "This is my third wine already. It's a good thing he drove, because I plan on not being able to drive later. This is what's going to get me through the night." She took one more sip. "In fact, I don't think I've driven at all in the last two weeks. Even Susan took us to the florists last, what was it, last Saturday?"

"The same day that Sandy was killed?" George asked quietly. The rest of the table had also gone silent, caught up in the conversation between the three of them.

"Yeah, that's right." Marcia stopped smiling and her speech was slightly slurred.

"So, your car has not been out of the garage all week?" George was staring at Jack, and Jack was returning the look.

"No, it hasn't. I should probably take it out tomorrow just to keep the battery alive."

"Good idea, Marcia. Jack, where's your book? I haven't noticed any at the table."

Jack's eyes never wavered. "It's probably around somewhere. I'll find it later. If I don't, I can always get another one."

Out of the corner of his eye, George saw Officer Seth Getty come in the front door, shaking off the rain. Following him was the newest officer, Carly Duncan. Sam came out of the kitchen, first looked toward George, then saw his brother and Carly, and went in their direction. He spoke with them for a few minutes, then handed Carly a plastic bag.

Marcia had continued talking, something about wanting to see a new movie now that the reunion committee no longer needed to meet, but no one at the table was listening to her. They were looking back and forth between George and Jack, Jack and George.

Carly and Sam came over to the table, while Seth headed to the back room. Conversations at the other tables now centered on the police officers rather than around each other.

Carly handed the package to George. "Mr. Peabody, Sam wanted you to see this first."

Sam added. "They found it under the, um, the, um, under ...."

George grimaced at the "Mr.", but decided now was not the time to insist on "George". He glanced into the bag, then back at Jack.

"Jack?"

Jack maintained his face expressionless for about twenty seconds, then suddenly deeply sighed.

"I was afraid that was where it was. I was hoping to get through the evening, but I guess I was lucky it lasted as long as it did." He looked down at the table.

Marcia looked confused. "Jack, what is going on? Is that your crossword book? Why are the police here?"

Susan put her arm around Marcia's shoulders. Betty got up from the other side of the table and took Marcia's free hand.

Jack shuddered and looked around the table before settling on George. "I assume you've seen what else is back there." George nodded. "I had wandered back into the kitchen just to see how the food was coming along – the smell was so tempting. Then I saw Gloria poke her head in the other door and smirk at me. No one else saw her, but that damn smirk got to me. After all the bad vibes from the committee, it was just too much. I pushed her back into the room and growled, 'Now what are you doing?' She pushed her chin out and said, 'You'll find out soon enough. Everyone will. Then we'll see who has the last laugh.' She had those packages against a table. I grabbed one and tore off the wrapper." He stared at the far wall for a minute. "You know what I saw." He brought his focus back to George. "I couldn't let everybody see that. It was meant to be humiliating, and it was going to be. It was bad enough that Sandy had kept throwing the Prom Queen and King thing up in Marcia's face.... I thought I had taken care of that problem last week." He threw his hands up. "This was supposed to be Marcia's night of success, and it was going to be, if I had anything to do with it."

George asked, "What about John?"

Jack shrugged. "I had nothing to do with that. I just saw how so much tension disappeared after he had died. But it was only a natural heart attack."

Everyone at the table sat in silence, not knowing what had just happened, but beginning to get a glimmer.

George nodded at Sam. "It's all you, now."

Sam took a breath and said, "We have just found Gloria Hramosky's body in the back room." He turned to Jack. "Jack Terry, we are arresting you for the murder of Gloria Hramosky, and as a person of interest in the death of Sandra Stillwater." He motioned for Carly. "Officer Duncan, read him his rights."

The rest of the room watched Jack being led out in handcuffs, then buzzed loudly with questions and wild suppositions. Marcia was crying as Susan and Betty accompanied her to the door.

Pete threw down his napkin. "I'll take care of this. I'll give a brief announcement regarding Gloria's death, and that the police are currently investigating the circumstances. And that's all we know."

As he went to the front of the room and raised his hand for silence, Fred whispered to Joe, "Have all your reunions been like this?"

Joe took a drink. "Not the ones I've been to. George, what happens now?"

George stood up. "I don't know about everybody else, but I'm starving. I haven't had anything to eat yet."

I'M TAKING THE LONG WAY

I'm taking the long way on my going home
For there's so much that I want to see.
The lights of the far town make me feel alone
But there's no place that I'd rather be.

The night falls so softly you can't see it fall
But the darkness provides its own light.
The stars may come out or they may not at all
But I'll still sing my songs through the night.

I'm alone with my thoughts, only time I can pause
Without worrying where they may go.
I don't want an answer, don't tell me because,
All I want is to think that it's so.

I'm taking the long way on my going home
For there's so much that I want to see.
The lights of the far town make me feel alone
But there's no place that I'd rather be.

If ... you receive a phone call by someone who purports to be The Almighty, do you think you had better say "yes" to whatever you are asked to do? Just in case?

CALLED BY GOD

Ring, ring! Ring, ring!

"Hello?"

"Yes, this is he. Who is this?"

"No, who is this, really?"

"God? ... You sound like Maggie from church."

"So, who is this ... really?"

"Again with the God. I have to say, you don't sound the way I would have expected."

"You know, more like James Earl Jones, without the Darth Vader mask."

"You get that a lot, huh?"

"Well, how about like my pastor, only with a deeper, more authoritative voice?"

"I guess not – that's not possible."

"Okay, I'll bite. So, you call yourself God. Is that a first or a last name?"

"Just God. That's enough for now –- the rest of it can wait till later?"

"So why are you calling me, God? Hah! Calling me God, hah, hah, that's a good one ... you get it? You can just call me –- "

"Okay, maybe we won't go there ... So why the phone call?"

"You are calling me to fulfill a greater purpose? To take on more of a leadership role in the Christian community? Uh-huh, are you sure you have the right number? This is –-"

"That's right. You've got the right guy. You know, I still say you sound more like Maggie, who's on all those church committees."

"You know, those church committees. Like, um, the worship committee, and the community service committee, and the nominating committee, and ... uh-oh ..."

"You want me to be on the church session, don't you? That's what this is all about."

"All right. I guess I can't say no to God. You got me for the next three years."

"What do you mean, the next six years?"

"Yeah, yeah. Okay. You have a good week, too. And I guess I will also see you in church, too."

If ... you have a friend with an obsession about spiders, would you stay friends with him or her? No matter what happens?

ANGELA

It was a Tuesday early in the fall semester when we first met Meriwether. Barney brought him up to our shared room and introduced him as a new kid that had just started at the university, and hadn't had a chance to make too many friends yet. Barney had, naturally, started talking to him in class and discovered that he was a collector of spiders. This, for whatever unearthly reason, was also Barney's consuming and everlasting passion, which now, after rooming with Barney for two years, had reluctantly become an interest of mine, too.

Thus, we were very excited about showing a fellow devotee our two newest acquisitions. We kept them in separate glass cases near the window for warmth. Every couple of days, one of us would drop in a few dead flies we had found on various windowsills throughout the dorm floor. Or, if we hadn't found anything, some mealworms that Barney got from a local pet store. But they preferred something still alive or freshly caught. The spiders would quickly spin a webbing around the victim, then take their own sweet time enjoying their breakfast.

We showed Lucretia to Meriwether first. She was the prize; the best one we had ever managed to catch. A gorgeous big Black Widow. Barney introduced her with the more formal Latin name, but I could never remember those classifications. Black Widow was enough for me. We had been very careful so far to keep her away from Lucifer, the top resident male spider.

Meriwether bent down to inspect her. "Now, that's beautiful. That really is." He looked back up at us and smiled. "Wish I could find a girl that I admired as much as that."

Barney was particularly anxious to show him Lucifer. A girl that we knew had discovered Lucretia in the guy's dorm, and had brought our attention to her by screaming, but Barney had found Lucifer on his own. When he looked down into the case, though, there was nothing to be seen.

"He's not here, Al!"

Meriwether and I leant over the cage and I swore softly to myself. "I'm sorry, Barney, but it must have been my fault. I cleaned the empty fly shells out this morning and I left the lid off for a minute. Just long enough to throw them into the wastebasket. I didn't think to recheck Lucifer before putting the lid back on. He must have gotten out then."

Barney looked at me for a long moment, then slowly and reluctantly sighed. "All right ... but he can't have gotten far. He must still be in the room. I just hope somebody didn't set his books down on him." The look this time was out of the corner of his eye.

Under our books was the first place we looked. Before we started a more thorough search, beginning near the glass case, then working outwards in ever-widening circles. After an hour and a half spent in dusty spider-likely corners, there was still no sign of him, and we had to admit defeat. Meriwether seemed disappointed that he had been unable to see Lucifer, but he took one last admiring look at Lucretia and promised to bring any more arachnids if he found some.

That was in the beginning of fall quarter our senior year. We never found another Lucifer, but Meriwether brought us several fine specimens and our collection grew. We were tempted to mate Lucretia so that we could watch another generation grow, but neither Barney nor I had the courage to offer up an unsuspecting victim, and Meriwether didn't believe we had a male fine enough for her after the loss of Lucifer. But he kept searching until the end of October.

Meriwether had come in one morning to feed Lucretia a special rare treat as the weather had gotten colder – a big fat fly that had somehow gotten trapped in his room. Maybe it was again my fault for hurrying so I could lock up on my way to class, but it wasn't until late afternoon that we discovered the lid left slightly ajar.

Lucretia, too, had managed to disappear. And she must have been in a big hurry because she had left the fly untouched. Once again, a search turned up nothing, not even a trace of web left behind.

Barney made some crack about her being horny and desperate, and having to go out and get some, but Meriwether stilled him with a look that I had never seen before on his face. A look of anger and pain and disappointment, so intense that Barney began to stutter, then faded off into nothing. He quickly turned away and shuffled his feet, trying to speak again. "I, ... I..." He stopped for a moment. "I guess we'll have to start looking for another one. There must be more than one Black Widow around here."

Meriwether spoke, his voice shaking, "There will never be another Lucretia!" He turned around and strode out of the room, slamming the door behind him.

Barney and I looked at each other, not sure what we had just witnessed.

######

We didn't see Meriwether at all for the next two weeks – handing in papers, getting ready for exams, and the usual school necessities. It wasn't until the weekend before finals that he came to our room again, this time bringing a young woman with him.

He introduced her as Angela and explained that they had met in a bar the week before – that she had come up to him and introduced herself. She was tall and slender, with long black hair and a full mouth, and I had to admit that she had a haunting, mesmerizing attraction. But it was a cold beauty. The pale skin was soft to behold, but ice to touch. The dark, piercing eyes looked right through me, freezing me to the spot.

Meriwether showed her the cases where we had kept Lucifer and Lucretia. She seemed more than mildly interested in them, and when she came to Lucretia's case, her hand darted in and found an old empty shell of an already devoured fly. When she saw it was empty, I could have sworn that disappointment touched her eyes for a moment. I glanced over at Barney, but he was busy showing off the rest of his collection and hadn't noticed a thing. I decided it must have been my imagination.

However, when they had gone, Barney shook his head. "Poor Meriwether. I hope he doesn't get stuck on her. I mean, it's okay now, but if he gets too involved with her, I don't know. She gives me the creeps."

We began to see Meriwether a little more often again after that, and more and more often we would see Angela with him. They became virtually inseparable and soon Barney and I were the ones making excuses not to see them, for neither of us had attained any great liking for Angela. Frankly, we were somewhat frightened of her. Whenever she was near, my skin started to itch, and my pulse began to pound, and it was all I could do to speak evenly. One evening Barney told me he had experienced the same sensations, but had considered it prudent not to express them. Apparently, Meriwether had apparently not felt any of this, for he, as Barney put it, "got stuck on her".

It was with dismay, but not any real surprise, that we heard of their engagement at the beginning of spring quarter. They planned to get married the first week in May and asked Barney to be the best man. He was reluctant at first because he doubted that he could generate the necessary enthusiasm, but he decided to go through with it for Meriwether's benefit. We had a few talks with the potential groom about just how sure he was of what he wanted to do, but he never wavered. He insisted he knew what he was doing, and there was no question in his mind about Angela's desire for him.

There was no question that she wanted him. As the day drew closer, she became even more attached to him, and, during the day, she wouldn't let him out of her sight for more than a few minutes at a time. Barney noted that she seemed to be awaiting her wedding night with a certain unusual relish. A hungry anticipation even.

It wasn't the typical wedding. Meriwether had previously told us that both of his parents had died when he was young, and the uncle who raised him was very ill and unable to come. But I was interested in meeting Angela's family. As head usher, I watched very closely for any family resemblance, but by the time the ceremony began, only students were present, and strangely enough, all friends of Meriwether's. Barney must have known that no parents were going to show, for he was the one to escort her up the aisle and present her to the groom. The wedding itself proceeded smoothly until the final vows. The minister turned to Meriwether and said, "Do you, John Meriwether, take this woman, Angela Aranea, to be your lawfully wedded wife?"

Meriwether had begun to pale about midway through the service and Angela had to prod him in the ribs before he responded with a small, "I do". The minister then turned to her, "Do you, Angela Aranea, take this ..."

From my position at the side of the chapel, opposite the congregation, I distinctly saw her lick her lips before an emphatic "I do."

After the small cookies-and-punch reception, I had an appointment elsewhere and didn't get back to the room till after dark, hurrying through a heavy rain. I smiled slightly as I thought that rain was supposed to be good luck for a bridal couple. Maybe I had been wrong about the whole thing.

I had left Barney to say the last farewells to the couple before they left for a brief honeymoon before returning for final exams. Thus, I was more than slightly surprised to see Meriwether's car sitting in the parking lot. I thought maybe he had forgotten something, or needed to talk to Barney about getting notes in class. I didn't spend too long outside speculating about it though. The darkness was becoming more and more complete and the driving rain pushed me into the building. I hurried in and up the stairs to our floor.

I got to our door and reached for the knob when I realized the door was already ajar, but there was no light coming from the room. It wasn't like Barney to have gone and not locked the door, let alone leave it open. And he liked to have the lights on at all times unless I was in bed. I could hear the rain coming in through an open window as I slowly eased through the doorway and groped for the light switch.

Before my hand reached the switch, though, lightning lit up the room and the scene flashed before my eyes. Barney lay stretched out on the floor, moaning slightly, blood oozing from the back of his head. A baseball bat was propped against the bed next to him. Next to Lucretia's cage stood Meriwether and Angela. They had not yet noticed the door opening, and, even as my fingers finished flipping on the switch, Meriwether did not appear to be aware of my presence. A blankness draped his face completely as his eyes focused only on Angela's.

But she knew I was there. She glared at me with more pure malice and hate than I have ever seen before or since. Then she was gone. Disappeared right in front of my eyes. Something small and black and squirming appeared in Meriwether's outstretched hands. He leaned over the case and set it gently down inside. Then he too suddenly vanished.

I moved slowly, unsteadily toward the case, listening to the rain pounding against the side of the building, feeling the dampness of the air coming through the window, and looked down into it. Lucretia had returned, and with her, finally, a suitable mate.

My gaze lasted for only a second, then I unhurriedly stepped over Barney and grasped the blood-stained bat. I held it vertically over the case and brought the thick end down upon them. Blood spurted for an instant, but it was confined by the glass. The wind rose and filled the room just then, amid a low rumbling of thunder. I went to the other cases and counted all of our remaining spiders. Then I deliberately crushed every single one while the rain continued to fall.

If ... you share lodgings with a famous detective, but you suspect he is keeping important information from you, wouldn't you try to solve the mystery? Using whatever means at your disposal?

THE ADVENTURE OF
THE MISSING CHOCOLATES

As I sat perusing the morning edition of *The London Times* over the remains of the excellent breakfast prepared by Mrs. Hudson, I could not help but recall that it had been quite some time since Sherlock Holmes had refilled the study candy dish, shaped, for Holmes' personally morbid reasons, as a skull. In fact, if memory serves me correctly, not since the winter of 1883.

There had been times in the past when the candy skull had gone empty for days, but Holmes' cravings had inevitably prompted him to refill it with mouth-watering chocolate creams, or whatever delectables struck his fancy at the moment. However, as I presently viewed his countenance, he appeared to be at ease – in fact, to be contentedly chewing. And yet, I was aware that we had completed the meal some fifteen minutes previously.

"Holmes!" I queried. "May I ask what you have found to continue to satisfy your appetite?"

But he remained unperturbed.

"My dear fellow, surely you are familiar with my methods. Eliminate the impossible, and whatever remains, no matter how improbable, must be the truth. Since there have been no chocolates in the skull for some time, nor any other edibles apparently present in this room, be assured that I must be merely sucking the remains of the good Mrs. Hudson's delicious omelette from between my teeth."

It was a perfectly plausible explanation, which was marred only by his then licking his lips.

I turned to the skull, bringing to mind the various confectionary delights, which had, at one time or another, been among its contents. The butterscotch chews, a popular item for clients being told their case was not of sufficient interest to engage our services. The cherry cordials, dripping on the Persian rug, presented to us by the Prince of Siam in gratitude for solving the scintillating adventure of the curious curry. And, of course, the cashew, mint-flavored chocolates, which constantly tempted the palate of our arch-nemesis, Dr. Moriarty. We had found it impossible to keep the skull filled when the doctor was on the prowl. The reader is, of course, familiar with these previous exploits of Sherlock Holmes, as his fame has spread from kitchen to bakery, from bistro to café.

But now, I found myself looking upon him with great suspicion. No secrets had heretofore been kept between us. Yet I feared some schism had developed. It was obvious to even such an amateur as I that he had availed himself of a chocolate from some hidden booty.

But where? Where would he have kept such a secret treasure? I prepared to use my powers of observation that Holmes had so often ridiculed.

I first considered the slipper upon the mantel. But I quickly dismissed it as I had, on occasion, passed within smelling distance of it, and could not conceive that anyone would willingly eat anything that had been confined within it.

The violin case in the corner next caught my eye. It was certainly large enough to contain a veritable bounty of sweet tidbits. However, it sat next to the heater, and I had difficulty believing that any chocolates would have survived to the point of being eaten by hand.

The last possible hiding place appeared to be the bottom drawer of the desk at which he now sat. The only way to determine the veracity of this hypothesis was to actively search the drawer.

I moved to the window, searching for inspiration. I needed to move Holmes away from that desk. A slow-moving animal came into view on the street below and reminded me of a previous case involving a missing leg of mutton.

"Holmes, there is a mysterious dog at the corner, and the more mysterious issue, as you have frequently remarked, is that it is not barking."

At once, as I knew he would, Holmes sprang to his feet and promptly fell over a small ottoman. He regained his footing and moved to the window to peer at the misbegotten creature.

Behind him, I strode quickly to the desk and pulled open the suspicious drawer. It was filled with chocolate – chocolate creams, nougats, chocolate mints, nut-filled chocolates, double chocolates, Willy Wonka Chocolates, chocolate bars, chocolates that had not even been invented yet.

"Aha!" I cried.

Without turning, Holmes calmly replied. "Please close that drawer, my fine friend. You know that I would not maliciously keep treats from you, but I have given my word to a young woman of my acquaintance that I alone would savor these in her memory. This was a case with which you are unfamiliar, involving a trapeze and whipping crème." He turned to again face me. "As for the dog that is not barking, there is a simple explanation. It is not a dog, but a giant rat, apparently from Sumatra."

I accepted his explanation with ill-humour, but little choice (I genuinely thought it was a peculiar canine). However, there will come a time when he will have to leave that drawer unprotected. I can wait. Maybe.

CAN YOU SEE WHAT I MEAN?

Can you see what I mean
When I say I can't be seen
For the time hasn't come yet to see me?
I'm alone in my world
With no banner unfurled
For there's nobody else wants to be me.

There's a song that I sing
But what good can it bring
For no one has ears with which to hear me.
But the words still will come
For the time they will not run
But as for now, all they know is to fear me.

I need a place to begin
But at the touch of my skin
The warmth of their bodies cannot feel me.
The time still runs on
Soon the moment will be gone
And they still will not know the real me.

Soon we hope to return
And may we all have learned
That there's more joy in a life that is shared.
Now we fly to the sun
With the dream that we are one
And know in our hearts that we all cared.

Can you see what I mean
When I say that now I'm seen
This is the time for us all to see me.

If ... you happen upon a veck who appears to be lost, try to avoid engaging it in conversation. There really is not much point to it ....

THE ARDOR OF THE LOST VECK

There used to be a time called wuncepona. It was named after Sam Wuncepona, who used to repair clocks down the street. He didn't charge much, but he did ask a favor of each of his customers, that they use the term "wuncepona time" whenever they were asked to pass the time of day. He figured it would save on advertising. It worked very well for a while. People would say, "What wuncepona time is it?", "It's almost wuncepona time for supper", "There's not much wuncepona time left in the game", and so on.

This went on until people realized why Sam didn't charge very much to fix clocks – he wasn't very good at it. Wuncepona time was never the same wuncepona time anywhere in town. 7:00 in the morning at the McGnats might be 7:01 at the McItches, or 6:30 at the McScratches, or even 7:00 in the evening at the McRubs. So, Sam's clock repair service ran down (he now removes peas from mattresses) and the people stopped referring to wuncepona time except in the past tense. It now refers to events that happened in the long ago, and better not happen again. The moral of this short parable is to never set your clock on anything but the mantel.

However, this has nothing to do with the present story. It is not set in wuncepona time, but is as far away as possible. The story concerns itself with a lost veck and its unfulfilled ardor (i.e. passion) for enlightened conversation. A veck, for those of you who have not experienced enlightened conversation, resembles nothing that you have ever seen before, or will care to see again. It is large enough that you have to step over it or around it, but small enough that you don't really mind too much. A veck walks on all fours, ... or sixes, ... or elevens, depending on the season. It can be fooled into thinking the season has changed by pouring seasoned salt on it, but only if it's still alive. If it's dead, the trick doesn't work. It is covered with short bristly hairs, which resemble a putting green more than anything else. It has two deep-set eyes, one on each side of its head, which makes it difficult to sneak up on. However, it can sneak up on anyone else without knowing it. In fact, the greatest danger that a veck can pose is running into you by mistake, and sticking its noses into your lunch.

This particular veck looked, oddly enough, much like most other vecks. He had not been reminded of this resemblance for several days, though. He had become lost when he sat down facing his family and did not realize when they had wandered off. Being lost was not particularly upsetting to him (it's hard to miss the company of vecks) so, having an unfulfilled ardor for knowledge and enlightened conversation; he set off to see what he could of the world.

He had not gone far (as vecks go) when he came upon a flower of the speckled dalliantrum family. He sat carefully down next to it, but not facing it, and spoke.

"Flower. Yoo-hoo, flower."

Now, a talking veck was the last thing in the world that this specific speckled dalliantrum had ever expected to see. She'd always thought that this sort of thing only happened to other dalliantrums, speckled or non-speckled. Her initial reaction was very similar to what yours or mine would be – she didn't know what to say. Fearing where the conversation might lead, she merely said, "Yes?", and instantly regretted that she hadn't said "No".

The veck now turned so that his other eye was toward the flower. He hoped it was still the same flower and hadn't moved during the shifting.

"I beg your pardon, Ms. Dalliantrum. I don't mean to bother you and I hope you don't think I'm rude ..."

Why wasn't I picked yesterday, thought the flower. But outwardly she merely nodded, in the way that flowers do and elevators don't.

"I am off to see more of the world," which is an odd statement for a veck to make, as they see twice as much of the world as anybody else at one time, "and I am searching for enlightened conversation. Could you point some out to me?"

"Why wasn't I picked two days ago?" said the flower, now out loud.

The veck assumed he was supposed to answer that question and he responded as vecks do to any questions asked of them. "I don't know." Vecks are known throughout the world as being whizzes at asking questions, but thoroughly useless at answering them. When they stay at home, vecks don't learn very much. Actually, even when they leave home, they don't learn much, but it's not as very.

At this point, you and I would probably give up on this conversation as being one of the lostest causes (most lost doesn't sound right either) that ever existed and leave. The speckled dalliantrum would certainly go along with that and, in fact, reached two of her petals down to try to pull herself out by the roots. I'm afraid that all she succeeded in doing was wrinkling her petals, which forever destroyed her chances of being picked.

"What do you want from me, veck? Give me your tired, your poor imagination. Regale me with your wisdom. Besiege me with your tiny particles of ingrained ingratitudes. Set my inner sanctuaries aflame with ambitious enthusiasm. Lift my alcohol-induced veil of insensibility. Ransack what's left of my little grey cells. Charbroil my ..."

"Oh, I like that." The veck sat back and clapped his front foot/feet together. "Those are really neat-sounding words. Is that enlightened conversation?"

"You want a neat-sounding word? 'Gonorrhea.' Just listen to that – 'gon-o-rrhe-a'. That's one of the most musically profound words ever spoken." The flower sighed, in the ways that flowers do and elevators don't. "But no, that is not enlightened conversation. However, it is the best that I have to offer you. Being a flower, an artistic object, so to speak (don't laugh), I can only present metaphorically and have to leave the enlightenment to the viewer. In your case, I think that's going to cause a lot of problems. Good day, and don't come back till I've been picked."

The speckled dalliantrum then attempted to close its petals in the way that elevators do and flowers don't.

The veck continued to wander, wondering. Or wonder, wandering.

The next time it stopped was in front of ... to the side of ... whatever, near to an owl in a lumium tree. It sat sideways (the veck, not the tree).

"Yoo-hoo, tree, owl, ... owl, tree." Having been raised among vecks, he was not quite sure which objects were capable of responding, and which were not, as evidenced by his conversation with a flower.

"Yes?" The pause was not as long this time. Throughout the following conversation, the veck was never really sure whether he was talking to the owl or the tree. In case you are wondering yourself, it was the owl. We both know trees can't speak veck.

"Do you have a name that I can use to call you?" asked the veck. "So that I don't have to keep calling you Mr. Tree-owl, or Owl-tree, or Towl-ree?"

"I am known as Abetakstello, an old and distinguished name, at least as far as I am concerned. What is it you want of me, my young veck?"

"I have an unfulfilled ardor for enlightened conversation. I have wandered far (for a veck) and a flower has informed me that I have not yet found what I desire. Maybe you can help me?"

The owl fluttered his wings, but, as that produced a rustling of the surrounding leaves, the veck was still not sure who had caused what.

"I am afraid I will not be able to help you much, either. Though I am an owl, my conversation is very limited for one of my species. I cannot ask the sort of questions that I am supposed to ask. I can say what, where, when, why, and how. But I cannot say what all the other owls can say, ... you know, ..."

"What?"

"No."

"No?"

"Yes."

The veck sat back, in the way that vecks do and nothing else does, and scratched where a neck might have been.

"I'm confused. You said you can't say 'what'?"

"No, I can say 'what', I just can't say, you know ..."

"You just said 'you know'."

"No, I didn't."

"Yes, you did."

"What did I say?"

"'You know'."

"No, I don't."

The veck scratched the other side of where his neck might have been. "Where were we?"

The owl smiled. To the veck's confusion, so did the tree. "Now, I can say that."

"What?"

"No."

"No?"

"Yes."

The veck sighed. Something he had learned from the speckled dalliantrum. Now, not only did he not know who he was talking with, he had completely lost track of what he was supposed to be talking about.

"I'm still confused."

"So are many that stop beneath this tree."

"Oh, who?"

"Right!"

"Right?"

"Yes."

"What?"

"No."

"No?"

"Yes."

The veck gave up scratching. Now he itched all over.

"Is this enlightened conversation?"

"Do you feel enlightened?"

"No."

"That's what I was afraid of. No one ever does. They usually just wander off again with a dazed expression on their faces. It's not very encouraging. I just wish I could say what other owls do, you know, . . . "

The veck showed that he had learned something after all on this trip, and left before the familiar dialogue could continue.

His ardor for enlightened conversation was still unfulfilled, but it had certainly been turned down low. He had almost begun to regret having gotten lost. Almost, but not quite.

The veck continued to walk, watching. Or continued to watch, walking.

The veck stopped next to a rock. The rock sat in the middle of the path minding its own business, not even acknowledging the veck's presence, but, as you probably could have guessed by now, this did not discourage the veck.

"Hello, I am a veck. I have an unfulfilled ardor for enlightened conversation. I am trying to learn about the world." Pause. Getting no response, the veck naturally assumed he was supposed to continue. "For example, I am very curious about your role and your thoughts about life. What are you doing now?"

The rock said nothing.

The veck thought that was interesting and continued his questions. "How old are you?"

The number of words that the rock used to respond was zero.

"Do you have any hopes or dreams for the future?"

The rock's response was nil.

"What is the greatest virtue that a being can possess?"

The rock answered with silence.

For once, the veck decided to quit before he found out he was behind. He was not confused (too much) at this point. He hoped there was more to life than the answers that he had just received, but, for the moment, he wasn't going to argue.

"Goodbye," he said to the rock and left.

The rock rolled over and laughed.

By now, the veck had wandered in a big circle and found himself back where he had started. Sure enough, the rest of his family was right where they had left him. Or where he had left them. One or the other.

"Hello!" he shouted. "I have found you again. I have been wandering, trying to satisfy my unfulfilled ardor for enlightened conversation. But I have been unsuccessful. I have not been able to hold a meaningful dialogue with anyone."

The two nearest vecks turned sideways to him so they could see him better.

"Mgbgg," they said. "Nllpppp, mggdmm."

"Now that's what I wanted to hear," said the veck happily.

The moral of the story is to know what you're looking for before you find it.

Alternative moral – never ever talk to a speckled dalliantrum, an owltree, or a rock about anything more serious than the weather or politics.

THE END

If ... you are called in to investigate a series of murders in a British community, make sure to keep track of the number of bodies. Remember, there can be only so many suspects left ....

THE MYSTERY AT
LITTLE OAKS MANOR

"Sir, there are already six dead bodies!"

"Already, Constable Sims?" Inspector Alistair Milrose-Plummett, holding his cane high for effect, stepped through the front door of Little Oaks Manor, the legendary home of Lord Percy Blather-Smythe, known for making his fortune through marketing Blather-Smythe birdhouses ("Where birds rule the roost"). "Are you anticipating more?"

"Well, sir, you know how these cases are." Constable Hannibal Sims wiped his muddy boots on the probably very expensive hall carpet. "Every time we show up, there seem to be more bodies afterwards than before."

"Be positive. Six seems to be a large enough number." Milrose-Plummett looked around the expansive hallway, noting the many grand portraits high on the walls, supposedly depicting multiple generations of royal Blythe-Smithers, though the current Lord had been the only one. A closer look revealed that they were all the same man, dressed in different period costumes. "Where are the suspects, I mean the survivors?"

"Sir, the rest of the household is gathered in the parlor. As usual. There is Lord Percy, his wife, Lady Priscilla, the two remaining children and heirs, Llewellyn and Belynda Blather-Smythe-Jones, the butler, Smith, and a cousin, Angus Porcbellough."

"So, still an even six left?" The inspector swung his cane around his left index finger. He didn't need it, but felt that it added an extra degree of intimidation when facing suspects, er, survivors. "That matches up well. Tell me about the victims. The ones so far, if your assumption is to be proven correct."

Sims pulled out his official Wobbly-On-The-Green police notebook and flipped through most of it before finding the right page.

"The information that we have so far tells us that the oldest son, Llionel, spelled with two L's at the beginning but only one at the end, was found hanging in his closet, when the maid went to hang up his trousers from the previous evening. The afore-said maid, Miss Juniper Lockbush, ran out screaming and tripped over a wire strung across the upstairs hall, falling down the stairs and breaking her neck. Angus' mother, the venerable Aunt Matilda, hurried out of the music room, where she had been practicing the harmonica, and was struck from behind by a mace taken from the suit of armor just outside the door, crushing the back of her head in. The gardener, Frances Rose, rushed in from the connected greenhouse, apparently saw something, and started to run back out, but was shot with an arrow from behind."

"You didn't need to say, 'crushing the back of her head in'. 'Crushing the back of her head' would have sufficed." Milrose-Plummett was keeping track of the deaths by counting them off on his fingers. "That's four. And the other two?"

Sims referred back to his notebook. "Apparently, the youngest daughter, Millicent, having watched all this from the upper balcony, reportedly fainted and fell over the railing to her death, crushing the top of her head, er, not in."

"Reportedly?"

"Well, she may have been thrown off, but her mother, Lady Prunella, stated that Millicent was always fainting at very minor disturbances, so she thinks it was also likely in this case. Anyway, that's what her mother said. Sir."

"One more?"

"After all this had happened, and the police were called in, we discovered Angus' father, Uncle Mortimer, on the floor on the other side of the bed in Llionel's room, with a knife through his heart. No one had thought to look for him before, as he usually spent a great deal of time on the, um, throne, if you take my meaning. He must have been the second, or even the first death."

Milrose-Plummett had stopped to lean on his cane throughout this report. "Thank you, Sims." He noted the bloodstains throughout the front hall from the various deaths, and reflected that the resale value of this carpet was probably now very low, except to a collector of memorabilia from violent crimes. "I think we should probably go now to face the remaining family." He resumed twirling the cane to make the grand entrance. Sims, very carefully, stayed at least two steps behind him.

They entered the parlor, and Sims quietly moved a vase before the twirling cane could find it. The family was engaged in playing a six-handed game of Whist, the Romanian version the inspector noted, and they waited for Smith, the butler, to make a play before they turned to their guests.

"Oh, company!" tweeted Lady Priscilla. "Smith, could you please get Juniper to fetch some tea for our new arrivals?"

"Madam, Juniper is dead." As everyone else's attention was currently on the officers of the law, Smith casually slipped a card from his hand to the bottom of the deck. When no one else said anything, he sighed and rose. "I suppose I shall have to take their coats and bring the tea."

"Gentlemen." He held the cane while the other two removed their outer garments and handed them to him. "Please have a seat." He left the room and deposited the coats somewhere out of sight.

Angus turned back to the card game. "Whose turn is it, eh? Mine?'

Milrose-Plummett nodded to Sims, who clapped his hands, gaining the attention of everyone at the table. Most of them, anyway. Angus was trying to peek at the hands of those closest to him.

"I am Inspector Alistair Milrose-Plummett, from Scotland Yard. I believe you have already met Constable Sims. We are here to investigate the deaths of six...." He turned to Sims for confirmation. "Yes, six members of your household."

"Six?" Lady Priscilla interrupted. "I thought there were only five."

Belynda set her cards face-down. "You've forgotten Uncle Mortimer again, Mother."

"Isn't he in the washroom?"

"No." Llewellyn rolled his eyes. "Not this time."

"Oh, my." Lady Priscilla fanned herself with her cards, looked them over, selected one to lay down, then fanned herself some more.

"Mother." Belynda rose from her chair and moved to the sideboard. "I believe you could use a brandy before you decide fainting would look lady-like about this time." She poured one from a decanter for her mother, then added a glass of her own. She returned to her seat and took a big gulp. Her mother glanced at her glass, but declined to touch it yet.

"Inspector." Lord Percy spoke for the first time. "Did you have something you wanted to ask us? I have rather a good hand and would like to return to the game."

"Ahem." The inspector cleared his throat. "First of all, I would like to know the whereabouts of each of you during the times in question, from when everybody retired last night through the later deaths in the front hall."

"Surely, you can't suspect any of us!" The Lady fanned her face more vigorously.

"Lady Penelope, I don't know anyone named Shirley here. But, yes, I do suspect each and every one until they have been eliminated as a suspect, one way or another. Let's start with you."

Sims pulled out his notebook in preparation for taking verbatim notes on the interviews.

"Ma'am, could you please tell us where you were last night and this morning?"

"I was in bed."

"All night?"

"Yes, of course."

"Alone? Can anyone corroborate this?"

"Well, the dog, Lancelot, sleeps with me. I'm sure he will inform you that I did not leave his side."

"And this morning?"

"Juniper brought me my breakfast about ten o'clock, as usual. A full English, with three eggs, two slices of toast, four rashers of bacon, sausage, black pudding, white pudding, tomatoes, and mushrooms. Oh, I just realized I did not have my scones. Where was Juniper's head? I will have to talk with her."

"Juniper is dead, Mother." Llewellyn spoke because his sister didn't. Everyone looked in Belynda's direction, because it was always her position to correct her ladyship when needed.

Belynda's head was face-down on the table. "Wake up." Llewellyn gave her shoulder a shake. Her head rolled to the side and her open eyes stared at nothing in particular. Angus, to the left of her, took a peek at her cards.

"Belynda!" Lady Priscilla snapped. "It is not nice to play dead in front of our guests. Sit up at once."

Sims moved to the table and felt for a pulse in her neck. "She is not playing, madam. She really is dead." He and the inspector looked at each other. "Seven."

Milrose-Plummett counted the remaining in attendance, then included Smith, who had just reentered the parlor. "Five left."

Smith was carrying a tea set with eight cups. He sighed and removed one, placing it on the sideboard. "Tea is served."

"Oh, I'll have one, with cream and two sugars, if you please." Angus excitedly spoke out.

"I'm fine with this." Lady Priscilla picked up her glass of brandy and downed it quickly.

"Lady Brunhilda!" The inspector raised his cane in her direction, but it was too late. She looked at him quizzically, then her eyes rolled back in her head, and she slid out of her seat and under the table.

Sims bent down, and after a few seconds, called out, "Eight," from under the table.

"Are you sure?" Lord Percy asked. "She never could hold her brandy. There's actually a pillow for her under the table for when this happens."

Sims stood up. "She is dead." The butler removed another cup from his tray.

Milrose-Plummet stamped his cane on the floor. "I believe we can safely say that the brandy is poisoned."

Sims raised an eyebrow. "Safely?"

"You know what I mean." He faced the remaining four. "Now, who would have set out the brandy?"

Smith said, "That would have been Juniper, the maid, sir."

"Bollocks! Or words to that effect." The inspector looked around the room and realized there were no women left to be offended. "We'll stick with bollocks. Did anybody see anyone alone with the brandy in this room since early this morning?"

"Um, sir. If anyone was alone in this room, then there would have been no witnesses to them being here. Alone. Sir." Sims shuffled his feet deferentially.

Smith set a tea down in front of Angus. Angus eyed it suspiciously, then pushed his seat back. "I think I could use some fresh air." He exited through the outer door to the garden, still holding his cards.

The butler held up the teapot. "Would anyone else be wanting some tea?" When everyone shook their heads, he sighed again, and picked up the tray. "I guess I will be washing these up." He then left the parlor.

"Sims, perhaps it is time for us to study the original crime scene. Maybe it will produce some stirring in this brain of mine, hmm?" Before he exited the room, Milrose-Plummett pointed at the two remaining members of the family. "Don't anyone else leave this room. There appears to be enough of you already wandering around." Percy and Llewellyn looked at each other with growing suspicion.

As the two representatives of the legal profession entered the bedroom of the deceased Llionel, they found there was barely room to move around. All of the dead bodies had been placed on the floor, presumably to simply get them out of the way. And where there was not a body, there was a pool of blood. It was impossible to tell whose blood was whose. Llionel's body had been cut down at some point and laid on top of the bed. With the sash from his robe still around his neck.

Milrose-Plummett moved to the closet and looked up at what remained of the sash still wrapped around a high rod used for hanging cravats. "I suppose it is doubtful that he committed suicide, Sims?"

"With all the later deaths, doubtful indeed, sir."

"But it would have taken a stronger person, most likely a man, to have lifted the son up to this high a level."

"That does fit with who we have left, sir."

The inspector pointed at the mass of bodies. "I believe we already have the stories of how these people died, but let's take a look at Uncle Mortimer's body, the one that was stabbed."

As they moved to the other side of the bed, Sims happened to look out the window overlooking the patio at the back of the house. He stopped and said, "Nine."

Milrose-Plummett joined him, and they looked down upon the body of Angus Porcbellough lying upon the patio stones, blood slowly pooling around him, his cards scattered.

"Bollocks again. He was my favorite suspect, the distant relation who had to eliminate everyone else before the inheritance would come to him. Now we are down to three. We had better go down and sort out the scene."

Before exiting the room, they quickly viewed the body of Uncle Mortimer. "Yes, as reported. A dagger through the chest. Not much chance of surviving that." The inspector indicated Mortimer's eyes. "Looks surprised. Apparently, he saw it coming, but did not expect an attack from that individual, and had no time to react defensively. One thrust and it was done." He looked at Sims. "He knew his assailant."

"Sir, they all knew each other."

"See, as I said."

As they came out on the patio, they noted the scattered playing cards. One lay near the head of the deceased and was particularly blood-stained. Sims knelt down to examine the body more closely.

"His throat has been sliced, sir, apparently by this card next to him."

Inspector Milrose-Plummett picked up one of the other cards. "Ow!" He looked at his index finger starting to bleed, then put it in his mouth to suck it. "The edges of these cards are very sharp!"

"They must take their card-playing very seriously in this family." Sims stood. "The card used to kill him was the nine of hearts. Sir, do you think there is any significance to that particular card being used as the murder weapon?"

"Well, it is the ninth body. And they were all connected in one way or another. All part of the same family, so to speak."

Sims shrugged and murmured. "Or it could simply have been the most convenient card."

"Let's go find out if the remaining family stayed where I told them to. If they did, that may make identifying the murderer a little easier."

"The number of victims has certainly been narrowing the field of suspects, sir."

Back in the parlor, they discovered that the father and son were not to be seen, disobeying the inspector's orders.

"Anyway, Belynda and ..." Milrose-Plummett pulled up the tablecloth to peer under the table, "Lady Pilsbury are still here."

"Sir." Sims had gone to the far side of the room beyond the piano, to where windows looked out on the stables. "One of the men is also still here."

The lower body of a male from the shoulders down was hanging from the windowsill, the head trapped by the window having been closed down on the neck.

"I believe it is Llewellyn, sir. He was probably asked to look out at something just under the window. This is now number ten, if you were still counting"

"We need to find out where the other two are, and where they were when this happened, Sims. With only two suspects left, I think we are closing in on the murderer." The inspector rubbed his hands together. "Isn't this exciting?"

In the hallway, they came across Lord Percy, drying his hands.

"I am sorry, Inspector. I needed to use the facilities. And with Mortimer now gone, I wanted to take advantage of spending some time there. There were a few magazines I wanted to catch up on. Have you discovered anything new?"

"I am afraid that I have to tell you of two more deaths, Lord Percy. Angus Porcbellough, whose throat had been cut, was on the back patio, and your son, Llewellyn, is in the parlor. His neck was crushed by a heavy window falling on him as he looked out."

"Oh, my." Percy put a hand to his mouth. "Do you think they might have been accidents? There have been so many today."

Milrose-Plummett paused, as if considering the possibility. "Unlikely. Angus' throat was slashed from right to left, and he had been holding the cards in his right hand, which would have made it very difficult to have accidentally made that cut. And the heaviness of the window would have required two hands to hold it up, which Llewellyn could not have done and stuck his head out at the same time."

Sims raised his eyebrows, surprised at his boss' powers of observation, or maybe at his ability to make up these facts on the spur of the moment. Whichever, it impressed Lord Percy.

"Then it must have been the butler! It's always the butler who did it in these cases, isn't it? We should have guessed from the beginning." His lordship waved his hand vaguely to the right. "He may be in the kitchen as we speak! I must see what has happened in the parlor!" He ran through the open doorway.

The inspector and the constable went in the direction that Percy had pointed, eventually finding the kitchen after passing through the dining room, and the pantry, and the staff's dining area.

"Just how large is this manor, Sims?"

"This large, sir." Sims held his hands far apart.

They discovered Smith standing at the sink. Rather, leaning at the sink. His body was upright, but his head was under the soapy water filling the sink. Sims lifted the head up by the collar, took one look, then let it drop with a splash.

"Eleven, sir. He has been drowned."

"Ah ha." Milrose-Plummett straightened up. "I think we now know who has been responsible for these grisly crimes. Sims, call for a car to come pick up the guilty party. We have an arrest to make."

They returned to the now-familiar parlor. Lord Percy was sitting at the table, holding up his cards, looking around the table with a smug smile on his face.

"I have such a good hand. Would you like to see? There is no one else to show it to."

Inspector Milrose-Plummett took a seat at the far end of the table. "I believe you, Lord Percy. I have no need to see it." He took a deep breath. "We are here to arrest you for the deaths of eleven ...." He looked at Sims, who nodded. "Eleven members of this household."

"So, you don't think it was Smith, the butler, then?" Percy reluctantly laid down his cards. "How did you know?"

"Very simple. The process of elimination. You are the only one left alive. You must have been the one that killed the others."

"Oh, I guess so." Percy looked around the room. "When you put it like that, I guess it was easy." He set his elbows on the table. "You know, when you are the one that everyone else relies on for money, the one that had worked hard for every penny, making Blather-Smythe birdcages ('A bird's home away from its natural home') for the ever-demanding public, there is a constant demand for that money. My beloved Lady Priscilla always wanted more and more scarves to wear in public. The children now had more expensive tastes in everything, and my sister's family was always mooching here. We couldn't get rid of them. And the staff! The staff was expecting to get paid regularly, can you believe that?"

They heard the siren of an approaching police car.

"It is so much easier with no one else here. I can even use the washroom when I want to, instead of waiting. It had almost gotten to the point of my having to put in a second toilet." He shook his head. "Oh, the pressures."

They escorted Lord Percy to the front of the manor and saw him into the waiting car.

"Well, Sims." Inspector Alistair Milrose-Plummett clapped his hands together. "Another case successfully completed."

"Yes, sir." Constable Hannibal Sims nodded. "And even one left still alive. One of our better adventures so far."

If .... everybody else seems to be counting on you to pray for them, and it works, when are they going to learn to do things for themselves? If your prayers are working, why would they need to do anything differently?

WHEN PRAYERS ARE ANSWERED

After Reverend Dennis Johns unlocked the front door of the Church of Hope and Light, he spent a few minutes alone in his office, asking for strength and guidance in facing the day. Then, having done his part in spiritual preparation, he followed his routine of moving to the sanctuary to sit in silence, just opening his mind and letting God now speak to him.

This morning, however, he found one of his parishioners already sitting in a pew.

Dennis slid quietly into a pew several rows behind the man, not wanting to disturb him, but being present in case he was wanted. Maybe this was how God was going to speak to him today.

The man had been simply staring ahead, but he must have heard or felt another presence. He turned slightly.

"Pastor Johns." He nodded towards the minister.

"Good morning, Tom. I'm sorry. I didn't mean to interrupt your praying, or meditating, or whatever you were doing."

"No, no, I was just sitting. Thinking, I guess, but mostly sitting." Tom Delisle shifted over to his left. "You can come sit up here if you like. You're not interrupting anything."

Dennis moved up to the same pew. "Can I help with anything?"

Tom sighed. Deeply. "I don't know if it's something you can help with." He sat silently for a moment. "But maybe you can understand better than anybody else."

Dennis put his left arm over the back of the pew to better face Tom. "I can always listen."

Tom glanced at him, then turned back to facing the front of the worship area. Looking at the figure on the cross.

After a moment, he said, softly, "You have always told us that prayer was very powerful. Maybe the most powerful thing we could do."

"Yes." Dennis nodded. "I believe that. It's talking directly with God."

"How do you know when your prayers are being answered?"

"Well, that's a tough question." Dennis looked down at his hands. "My personal belief is that God is always listening, and that there is always an answer. It may not be the answer we were hoping for. And we may not even perceive an answer at all. But it is there.

"I believe life is to be lived, and choices are to be made, and sometimes things just happen. No matter what choices we make, or prayers we pray. If we got everything we wanted through prayer, it would be difficult to really appreciate what we do have. And we wouldn't have to work at things, like relationships, or goals, or accomplishments, or focusing on doing what is right …. Prayer isn't here to make life easy."

Tom looked him in the eye. "I think my prayers are being answered."

Dennis cocked his head. "Well, I would say that's a good thing. I know you are a good person, so I wouldn't expect you to be praying for something that is wrong."

"No, you don't understand." Tom's voice began to get louder and higher. "All of them. Every single time. Exactly the way I am asking."

"I don't know what you mean." The pastor frowned. "Again, I wouldn't have expected that, because that's not the way I believe prayer is supposed to work. But I would think you would be happy with those results." He paused. "But that's not what I am seeing from you. You don't appear to be happy."

"I'm exhausted." Tom clenched and unclenched his hands. "I'm praying for everyone. All the time. I don't dare stop."

Dennis took a moment to respond. "What are you praying for, Tom?"

The man looked to the cross again. "It started with praying for the families that had lost someone during the pandemic. We did that every Sunday in church." The pastor nodded. "And then for people I knew that had gotten sick. That they would get better. Do you know how the deaths suddenly seemed to stop about two months ago? Everywhere?"

Again, a nod. "But there have been a couple of days when a lot of people have died from the disease. A day here and there, just to let us know it was still with us."

Tom shook his head. "I was praying for everybody to be protected from the virus. Especially the ones not taking the vaccine. The first reoccurrence was a day I took off. I just didn't take the time to pray that day. But I resumed praying the next day and nobody died for several more days. I stopped another day to just to see what would happen. And then everybody started dying again. I haven't stopped since then." He took a deep breath. "And nobody else has died."

Dennis shook his head slightly. "Tom, there have been many people praying."

"I know, I know. That's what many of the unvaccinated are saying. That they don't need a vaccine because people are praying for them. Many of them are counting on prayers of others to protect them." Tom turned to Dennis. "But there's more. That's the only group prayer I'm doing. The rest are for individuals or families. My cousin, Betty, couldn't get into a hospital for a surgery she needed. I prayed, and she got the surgery the next day. I prayed for Mark Smith to get a job, and he found a job. Evelyn was on hospice and not supposed to survive the next day, and I prayed for her to get better. And she did. When was the last time we had a member of the congregation die? It's been months."

"Josie Fischer had that heart attack."

"I couldn't see that coming! It was so sudden, I couldn't do anything about it. But I have prayed for her family every day since then. As well as all the other families having medical or work or personal issues from our church. Every single one of them, individually. I tried to do a prayer that covered everyone. But that's when the Petersons separated, and a few were laid off from work, and my brother's cancer spread. I have to do each of them one by one. Every day!" Tom threw his hands up. "And it works. But I have to keep doing it."

Dennis had to take a few minutes to think of what to say next. "These things happen. I'm sure everyone appreciates your prayers, but sometimes, these things happen."

Tom produced a weary smile. "The Summerfield High girls' basketball team hadn't won a game in two years. Just to test the strength of these prayers, I prayed for them to win a game. They beat a team that hadn't lost all year."

"But ..."

Tom held up a hand. "I haven't prayed for anything for myself. Or for any other sports teams, or political contests. Though I must admit, I prayed for voters to use good sense in the last election." He shook his head. "I don't believe God is supposed to work that way. If that was the way prayer worked, all the teams and all the candidates would always win."

He sighed. "I'm tired. I'm adding new names every day. There are emails and messages, and people that I talk to, constantly asking for prayers for somebody. I haven't gone on social media in a long time because of all the prayer requests, and prayer chains, and 'If you love Jesus, pray for this'."

Neither man spoke, each alone with his thoughts. Finally, Dennis stirred.

"I don't know what to say, Tom. I'd offer to pray with you, but I don't think that's what you want to hear right now."

"It's not that there aren't people and things that I want to pray for or about. But I don't want to be responsible for everybody! I wish people would take responsibility for themselves. If you're sick, see a doctor. If you don't want to be sick, take the vaccine. If prayer comforts you, then do it. But don't rely on others to do it for you, just so you don't have to do what you know you should do. I don't want to do this anymore, but I don't dare stop."

"Tom, you're not responsible for everyone. People make their own decisions. Good or bad. That's what life is about. I am going to pray for you right now. For your care. I am going to pray that you find the strength and determination to do what is best for you. And that God finds a way to heal your troubled spirit and to let you know you can ease your burden."

Both men bowed their heads. Dennis knew he could never know what Tom was silently praying for right then, but he knew his prayers were for Tom's peace.

When Dennis looked up, he saw that Tom's head was still bowed. It remained that way for several more minutes. Tom finally shook himself and looked up.

"I'm sorry. While I was there, I thought of several other people to pray for. I keep adding to my list all the time."

Dennis put his hand on the other man's shoulder. "Tom, you are not alone in this. You have to know that this is not your responsibility to solve all the problems of the world. You do not have to do this by yourself."

Tom looked at Dennis for a few minutes. "I know what you're saying, Reverend Johns. But what if it is up to me? What if this is what I am meant to do? I can't take that chance to stop." He stood up. "Thank you for listening to me."

The pastor moved into the aisle to let Tom Delisle out. "Tom, you don't have to keep doing this."

The man grimaced, then started walking to the exit. "I guess this is between me and God. As prayer is supposed to be."

Pastor Dennis Johns watched him go, desperately hoping and praying that he could do something to ease Tom's burden. But he recognized that prayers aren't intended to always have a neat and tidy solution. He would have to trust in God.

A MAN WAS SITTING NEATH A TREE

A man was sitting neath a tree
And pondering said he,
"I've thought about what I must be,
I'm afraid I still can't see.

I've thought about why I've come,
The places I'm descended from.
I've had these thoughts and then had some,
I'm afraid I still can't see.

Are we to never know the why?
Why men live and why men die?
Howling winds may help us cry,
I'm afraid I still can't see."

A man was sitting neath a tree
And laughingly said he,
"I'm the greatest in history,
But I'm afraid I still can't see."

A man was sitting on a hill,
Said he, "Come help me if you will.
Of these days I've had my fill,
I'm afraid I still can't see.

My name was Peter, now they call me Paul.
They say I'm the greatest of them all.
I've seen many empires fall,
I'm afraid I still can't see.

I've lived many lives before,
Lived through peace and I've lived through war.
I still can't tell just what's in store,
I'm afraid I still can't see.

Jesus was the first they said,
Among the living and the dead,
A crown of thorns upon his head,
I'm afraid I still can't see.

I've had many names since then.
I've lived with many types of men.
I've lived in hell and I've lived in heaven,
I'm afraid I still can't see."

A man was sitting on a stone.
Said he, "I sit here all alone.
I've got nothing to call my own,
I'm afraid I still can't see."

I left that man sitting there,
Without a worry, without a care,
That he thought that he could share.
I'm afraid that now I see.

If ... you are home alone, and it starts to rain, do you ever pause and just watch the drops falling? And then do you have trouble not watching that one drop falling, over and over ... and over...

RAINDROPS

The man looked up from the book he was reading.

What's wrong with the radio? He then stood and moved over to inspect the old sound system, from which only static now came forth. The radio was a remnant from his youth that he refused to give up, no matter how much better the current audio systems were supposed to be. Glancing out the window, he saw the reason for the disruption in the music.

Why, it's raining out ... pretty steadily. And getting dark. A puzzled look crossed his face. *Why didn't I notice it before? Those clouds must have been gathering for some time. I know I had the radio and the light turned on, but you'd think I'd have noticed something.*

A fine rain, almost invisible, was coming down, but the man could see the drops splashing in the puddles that had already formed. He noticed a board lying near the house beneath the window, protected from the immediate downpour by the overhanging roof, but not from a solitary drip from the roof's edge, which landed regularly on its exact center. He watched for a minute or two as the ring of moisture spread slowly out from that center. It reminded him of the famed Chinese Water Torture. *It comes down regular as clockwork. One ... two ... drip. One ... two ... drip. Yep, regular as clockwork. I can see how that could really drive a man crazy, ... one drop at a time, every couple of seconds. You just sit and anticipate the next drop. Anticipate, fear it, pray for any difference in the pattern. I imagine one second could mean a lot to a man in that position.*

The man switched off the annoying radio noise and peered out into the growing darkness. *Looks as if it's here to stay for a while. I wish Beth were here. I don't like the idea of her driving in this weather. But she's a sensible woman. She'll put up somewhere till it lets up.*

He glanced once more at the board and saw that the moisture ring had expanded until it was about two inches in diameter. *I wonder if the board has a way of anticipating those drops. Each fiber in it is just waiting for the next drop, waiting expectantly to absorb it. I couldn't stand it. I know I couldn't. That waiting would get to me.*

The man went back to his chair and picked up the book that had been cast aside. He tried to read for a few moments, but then looked up again. Something else was bothering him. He seemed to be waiting for something, anticipating something. When it came, he knew it had come, but he did not know what it was, only that he must wait for it to come again.

What is it? There it is, and this time it became familiar.

Drip.

It's a dripping somewhere. But where is it coming from? Instinctively looking up after his thoughts of Chinese water tortures, he started to smile, but thought better of it.

Drip.

Where is it coming from? Where the hell is it coming from?

Drip.

He went to the window, but realized that the audible drip was not outside, but inside, in the house with him. He found himself waiting, not to determine where the sound came from, but simply in anticipation of the next drop.

Drip.

He walked into the kitchen to check the faucet there, but that was not the one.

Drip.

He hurried into the bathroom to check the sink and tub. It was not there.

Drip.

There's only one more place. It has to be the upstairs bathroom. That's the only place left.

Drip.

Frantically, he tore up the steps.

Drip.

A glance showed him it wasn't the sink.

Drip.

He ripped the bath curtains aside.

Drip.

I found it! But the handles on the faucet were already turned back as far as they could go.

Drip.

There must be some way for me to stop this damned dripping.

Drip.

His gaze swept around the small room. *The plunger! That's it, the plunger!*

Drip.

He propped the plunger up so that the end was stuck in the faucet and the other end was on the floor of the tub. Now the water would run down the plunger, but would not make a sound at all.

He waited for the next drop. *Please don't fall, please don't.*

It didn't. It simply dribbled down the plunger with no sound.

The man walked downstairs, shaking slightly and fumbling for a cigarette before he remembered that he had stopped smoking a month earlier. He passed by the window and smiled out at the board, laughing at it and the torture it was going through.

He had already gone by when he realized it. He turned back and stared at the board. The drops were still falling, but the moisture ring was still only two inches in diameter. *My God, the water's being absorbed inward now. It's boring down through the wood.*

He jerked himself away from the window. *I've got to get my mind off it, think of something else. I'll turn on the TV, that's what I'll do. Let's see what's on now.* He started to pick up the program listings, but threw it back down. *The hell with what's on. Anything will do.*

He turned it on and sat back on his chair. He wiped the sweat off his brow and set on the edge of the seat, nervously twisting his hands in his lap, trying hard to keep his mind on the screen.

Suddenly there was a violent boom of thunder and a crash of lightning, and both the lights and the television went off.

He sat there in the dark. *Oh, My God! No, this can't be happening to me! It can't be!* He started to the window. *No, I have to stay away from the window!*

But he couldn't.

He was drawn to the window and the simple but fascinating scene outside. The simple but fascinating scene of a drop of water falling. Not just falling, but falling on a board. Tormenting it and the man that was watching that simple scene. He stood there watching every single drop, anticipating it, fearing it, and praying for any possible distraction. One ... two ... drip. One ... two ... drip. And at each drop, he flinched as it fell. He could feel each one, boring into him, his mind blank except for quiet anticipation. One ... two ... drip. One ... two ... drip. One ... two ... drip ...

If ... you find yourself stuck in a room, and the only decision you have to make is whether to go through the solitary door or not, how long would it take you to make that decision?

THE DOOR THAT GOES NOWHERE

Should I, or shouldn't I?

I'm so lonely. It's so hard to be lonely, not to have a friend to talk to, to share with, even to care for. So hard. So hard to see nothing but four walls and a door that goes nowhere.

That's funny. A door that goes nowhere from nowhere. Because this is nowhere. I'm nowhere and I'm here, so here must be nowhere. And there's nothing out there. So that must be nowhere.

Now that's what I call a useful door.

I told him that once. I told him and I laughed because I thought it was funny. He gave me that strange look he has and wrote something in that book he carries with him. I said, don't you think that's funny? He said yes, but he didn't laugh. I've only seen him laugh once. That was when they first put me in here, and I asked him why the room was all white and there wasn't anything for me to sit on or lie on or anything. That was when he laughed and tried to tell me that the walls were painted a light shade of red and that there was a bed and a table and a chair.

At first, I thought he was crazy, but then I saw what he was trying to do. He was trying to make me think I was crazy. But it isn't going to work. I know I'm not crazy, and I know what I see. I mean, I know what I don't see. I don't see any red walls and I don't see anything in this room. No bed, no table, no chair. Nothing but a door. The door that goes nowhere. The door that goes nowhere from nowhere. That's funny. I tried to tell him that was funny, but he didn't laugh.

I don't remember anything from the other side of the door. There's nothing out there, so that's why I say the door goes nowhere. There can't be anything outside there or I would remember it. Wouldn't I? Shouldn't I remember something if there was something out there? But I don't. I don't remember anything, so there must be nothing. And if there's nothing, it must be nowhere. The door that goes nowhere from nowhere. From nothing to nothing.

Should I, or shouldn't I?

I haven't seen him for several days now. It's been just me and the door. And the air. The air is what I live on. I breathe the air and I eat the air. They won't feed me any food, so I have to eat the air. There's enough air to eat because it's pressed closer together in places in this room. In this room of nowhere. Some places it's pressed so close together that I can't move through it. I've tried to push through, but I can't do it. It's just like pushing against a brick wall.

He tried to tell me that was where the bed was, but I know better than that. There isn't any bed in here. I know. I have to sleep in the corner because they didn't give me a bed. If there was a bed, I'd sleep on it. I like beds. I always felt so warm and comfortable and safe in my bed at home. I wasn't lonely there. When I was in my bed at night, nobody was telling me what to do or what not to do. What to see or what not to see. I was somewhere then. I wasn't nowhere. I wish I had a bed here. I wouldn't feel lonely then. But they won't give me one. They said I've already got one. That's because they want me to think I'm crazy. But I'm not crazy. I know there's no bed here.

Should I or shouldn't I what?

I don't remember. I don't remember. I don't remember. I don't remember what? I don't remember what I should or shouldn't. Maybe I shouldn't remember. That would answer the question. Because if I don't remember, then I shouldn't remember, so that means that I shouldn't, should I?

But I can't. I can't remember.

There's a big bloodstain on the wall in front of me. It just appeared in the far top corner this morning, but it's been spreading all day. I've been sitting here on the floor in my corner all day long watching it spread. Coming down closer and closer to the floor. It's not dripping, it's just spreading, getting closer and closer, widening out as it's coming. Soon it will cover half the wall. Maybe it will start on the next one. It's a nice bright shade of red. Red – that's the color he told me the walls were. That would be funny, he told me they were red when they weren't, but now they are. I like the color red, but not blood. Not red blood. I wish it would go away, but it doesn't. It just spreads and creeps closer and closer, more and more. I'm afraid to go to sleep. Even down here in my corner. How far is it going to creep when I'm sleeping? I might wake up and find that it has crept onto me. That's a lot of red blood.

Two walls are completely covered now. I told him about it when he came in. For the first time in a long time, he smiled at me. I said, no, this isn't funny, don't laugh, I don't want the red blood creeping up on me when I'm sleeping. This isn't funny. He said he wasn't laughing, he was pleased at my progress, that he had told me before that the walls were red. But I know. He was laughing because he thought it was funny, that the walls were turning red like he said they were. I wish they would turn back to white. I don't like that red blood. That blood red.

I remember now what it was that I should or shouldn't. Should I or shouldn't I go through the door that leads nowhere? He has been trying to get me to go through that door, to see what's going on outside of this room. But I told him there's nothing out there, because that door leads nowhere. That door goes nowhere from nowhere. There's nothing out there, just like there's nothing in here, but they'll try and make me believe that there's more out there. But I know there isn't, I know. Should I, or shouldn't I?

All four walls are completely red from the blood now. That's an awful lot of blood. Red, red blood. He's happy now. He says I'm improving. But I'm not improving. I'm scared. Where did they get all that blood from?

They're trying to drive me crazy. They want me to think that the walls have been red all along, and I just couldn't see the red before. Oh, I know. I know what's going on. But where did all that blood come from?

Should I, or shouldn't I? The door. That's what it is, the door. Should I or shouldn't I go through that door? They want me to. They want me to go through that door into nowhere. Only they say it's not nowhere. I wish I had a bed. Then I could lie on it and sleep on it and feel safe. I wouldn't have to sit in the corner and look at the red walls then. The red blood walls. Why won't they give me a bed?

The walls are still red and there's a chair in the room. There's no chair in the room. There's a chair in the room. There's no chair in the room. There's a chair in the room.

They put it in last night. I know they did. He said it had been here all the time. But I know it wasn't. They put it in here when I was sleeping, not sleeping, dreaming, not dreaming about the red blood walls. The red blood walls creeping up on me. But it's not a bed. It's just a chair.

Should I, or shouldn't I?

They brought a table in last night. Now there's a table and a chair. Still no bed. Now there are four blood red walls, a table, a chair, and a door that leads nowhere. Somewhere. Nowhere. Four red blood walls and a door that goes nowhere from nowhere.

Should I, or shouldn't I? He said that's somewhere out there. Maybe there's a bed out there. Why don't they give me a bed? Why am I nowhere?

Should I, or shouldn't I?
I got a bed. I got a bed. I got a bed. I got a bed. I got a bed.
But I'm still nowhere. He said the bed's been here all the time. Has it? I know it hasn't. I know it ... maybe.

I'm still nowhere. I'm still in a room with a door that goes nowhere from nowhere. Cause I'm here and I'm nowhere. But where is somewhere? Does the door go somewhere? He said it does. He said it goes somewhere. Will it go somewhere? Will I be somewhere when I go through the door? I feel safe lying on the bed right now. I don't feel lonely. But they may take it out again and try to make me think that it's still here. Then I'll be lonely and afraid again and still nowhere.

Does it go somewhere? I want to be somewhere. All I have to do is turn the knob and open the door and go out. And leave nowhere. That's all I have to do.

Should I, or shouldn't I? I remember. I should. Whether the door goes somewhere or nowhere, it leaves nowhere. Am I going somewhere?

Goodbye nowhere.

If ... you are going with your mother on an obligatory trip to elderly rela- tives, and they don't have anything appropriate for a child to play with, maybe you might as well listen to some stories. What have you got to lose?

VISITING WITH UNCLE ALBIE

When I was young, probably somewhere between four and eight – I'm not very good with ages for when I did something, I just know I was smaller than anybody else, and that it was sixty-some years ago – my mom used to take me to visit her aunts, who were living with their uncle, her Great-Uncle Al- bie. I don't rightly know just how old any of them were, just that it made them my great-aunts, and Albie my great-great uncle. Or thereabouts.

Mom would go off to do something with Mabel and Bertha, while I sat in the front room with Uncle Albie. He didn't like all those greats in front of his name, so he was just Uncle Albie to me. That was okay. I'd have gotten tired of saying "great-great" all the time. The room was always dark, with the curtains drawn closed and only the one floor lamp behind him turned on. Our older neighbor's house was also like that. I never did figure out why some older people didn't like to have the sun coming in. Probably something with causing the furniture to fade. But you couldn't make out the color of the furniture in the dark, anyway.

It wasn't until my late teenage years that I figured out which aunt was Mabel (the shorter one) and which one was Bertha (the taller one). It was always just "We're visiting Mabel and Bertha", or "Mabel and Bertha are coming over", or "That birthday card is from Mabel and Bertha". Never just one of them at a time. Later on, when Mabel was having serious health problems and was in a nursing home, I got to know Bertha as herself. She was a hiker and a bird-watcher, and was kind of cool once I knew that.

Uncle Albie and I didn't have a lot in common. He asked me a few times if I played checkers, but he always cheated when we did play. He'd take two turns in a row or try to jump me from too many spaces back. We lasted only a game or two, which was about the limit of his willingness to play. He liked to talk, and, no matter what we started out doing, he soon was reminded of a time when he was younger, and off he'd go.

"I recall, when I wasn't much bigger than you, when me and my dog, Bo, would go down to the Mercantile on Main Street. Course there was only the one road going that way past the store, and I don't know what the name really was, but it was always known as Main Street. Maybe The Main Street. And the store was the Mercantile because it had a little bit of everything you'd ever need. Not a lot of stuff that you'll never use like you get in those big, fancy discounts now. I think it was Sweeney's Mercantile on the big sign up top, but Sweeney had sold out to a man named Douglass a while back, who never changed the name, so it was just called the Mercantile.

Anyway, Ma would send Bo and me down there every once in a while, to get some sugar or flour or butter, maybe, but I think it was more just to get us out of her hair, so she could get some things done around the house. Bo's full name was Bolivar, named after some general or president of some foreign country. Pa saw the name in a book he once read and liked the way it rolled off his tongue, but he was the only one ever used the full name, Bolivar. To everyone else, the dog was just Bo. Ma didn't mind if we were gone for some hours, just so long as we weren't under her feet.

The old men would hang around that store and play a lot of checkers, and I liked to watch. One of them, Calvin, would tell jokes that, normally, I was not allowed to hear, and I ain't repeating them for your ears, so don't ask. And he liked to cheat at checkers, particularly when he played Lucius, who was blind as a bat. And hard of hearing, to boot. Lucius could sort of make out the colors on the board, but not much else. Calvin would tell a joke to get Lucius' mind off the game, then jump three men that weren't anywhere close together. Hah, everything I know about playing checkers, I learned from watching Calvin.

Well, there was this one time, when Lucius' grandson was visiting, and was making suggestions to his grandpa on where to move his checkers. Calvin couldn't make his usual, not quite according to Hoyle, moves and it looked like he just might lose for once. He leaned back and spotted me and Bo standing off to one side. Now Bo had a weakness for licorice whips and, on good days, would manage to beg one off of Mr. Douglass, the shopkeeper. Calvin had seen this often enough to know what Bo liked. He reached into his pocket underneath the checkerboard table, and, unseen by anybody but me, pulled out a licorice whip, and snipped off just a little end of it. Of course, Lucius couldn't see it and his grandson was busy studying the board. But I watched Calvin wave it around just a bit under that table, just enough to get Bo's attention. It didn't take much and Bo was under that checkerboard, chawing down that piece of licorice and upsetting the whole table. Well, that was the end of that game, yessiree."

Uncle Albie reached for the glass of lemonade that was always sitting next to him, and took a sip. There was also a bowl of those hard candies that take a long time to suck down, and he offered me one. I always thought that the point of those candies for adults, was that it took so long to suck on that it kept you from eating too many. It wasn't my favorite, but it was candy, so I took it. He then took out a cigar and looked at me, tilting it in my direction as if about to offer it. I think it was just a gesture of habit, because he immediately shook his head and stuck it in his own mouth. Anyway, it was good I had that hard candy, anyway. He lit it up, took a deep breath, and blew the smoke out around his head. Right then, we heard a police siren go past the front of the house, and Uncle Albie chuckled.

"That reminds me of a time, Ma's brother-in-law, Eddie Gates, married to her sister, Clarice, bought the first car in the family. I was too young to know anything about what kind it was, only that it didn't need a horse to go, and that it went fast. The only other car we saw regular around there was the police car, and nobody let you get too close to that. It took me half an hour to walk down to the Mercantile, but only two minutes to get there in Eddie's new vehicle. He took me for a ride, just to show me how fast it could go. Ma was scared to death to let me ride in it and insisted that I had to keep the window up to make sure I didn't get blown out. But I did get tossed around whenever he'd take a turn, as fast and as sharp as he could. Sort of like being in one of those rides at the county fair, the kind that Pa always said not to tell Ma about.

Eddie pulled up in front of the Mercantile, throwing up a cloud of dust so thick, I couldn't see out the window. I know anybody out there couldn't see me, and probably not even the car. The shopkeeper, Mr. Douglass, came out on the front porch, as well as our local member of the police force, Officer Foster. The only time you ever saw Officer Foster was sitting at the counter in the store, sucking a grape soda out of the bottle with a straw. I think he was afraid if he tilted the bottle up to take a sip that he'd spill some on his uniform, which might give away where he'd been spending his time.

I take that back. I did see him once hauling a hobo out of Shaker's Woods, who old Miss Tucker swore was stealing pies that she was setting out to cool on her windowsill. Now, that hobo might have been stealing some of them, but I know there was one that he didn't take. My best friend, Joey Cramer, and I sort of borrowed that one cherry pie, just to taste, you know, and never got around to putting the rest back. Maybe we just finished it off, to hide the evidence, if you know what I mean.

Anyway, Officer Foster took a look at all that dust still hanging in the air, and calmly asked, 'You wasn't speeding, was you?' I nodded, but Eddie shook his head. 'Cause, if I catch you speeding, I'm going to have to haul you in.' Again, I nodded, and, again, Eddie shook his head. 'Just don't let me catch you, son.' This time, Eddie smiled and nodded. Not getting caught was the part he could agree to.

I don't rightly know what the speed limit around town was, or anywhere else for that matter, but I do know that Eddie never paid any attention to it. Specially if Aunt Clarice wasn't with him. He slowed down a little bit with her, cause her threats were going to mean something to him. But if she wasn't in the car, there was no limit. There were a couple of times we'd hear the police siren go by our house, and we'd know Officer Foster was trying to chase down Eddie.

As far as I know, Eddie got away with it, till one time we heard the siren, then a loud crash soon after. We came running out of the house, and found Officer Foster leaning on the front of his car, laughing at Eddie getting yelled at by Farmer Jones, who'd been delivering milk and eggs in his horse-drawn cart. Eddie had run onto the back of the cart, and there were broken milk bottles and scrambled eggs all over the road. The horse, Ol' Maggie, was in front, calmly chewing on some hay, but the farmer looked fit to bust and was letting Uncle Eddie really have it. Ma covered my ears, but I heard enough before she did. Eddie's car wasn't too damaged, but the back wheels on the cart were split off and the back end lay in the dirt, with more milk and eggs still sliding off. It was the beginning of the biggest breakfast you ever did see.

I don't know if Eddie ever got that speeding ticket, but I do know he had to pay for all of Farmer Jones' losses, and we didn't see him around town in that fancy car for a while. At least until several hard rains had taken care of that mess on the road."

By the time Uncle Albie had finished that story, his cigar had gone down to a stump. He tamped it out in an already pretty full ashtray. This time he took out two different hard candies from a pocket, gave one to me, and took one for himself, I think to take the taste of the cigar out of his mouth. He let the smoke around him sort of drift off, then took a sniff of the fresher air.

"I believe they have a soup going in the kitchen. Wait a minute, I bet I can figure it out. I think it's my favorite, ham and bean. Your mom and your aunts make some pretty fine soups. And, if I'm not mistaken, I can smell some sourdough biscuits to go with it. We're going to have some good eatin' tonight. I bet you're taking a good-sized batch home for your family for the next couple of days.

My Ma tried to teach me how to do some cooking. My sister, Sara, your great-grandma, took to it right off, but I never quite got the hang of it. I'd forget to peel the carrots, or clean the ham off the ham hocks halfway through, so there'd be these two big bones full of ham sitting in the soup at the end. I tried to get away with putting one of them in my bowl and pretending it's what I wanted to do all along, but Ma wasn't having none of that. And the biscuits.... Oh, Lord. I could never remember whether it was baking powder or baking soda I was supposed to put in. I just know one of them didn't work well at all. Nosiree. Those biscuits were as flat as a sheet of paper, maybe two sheets put together, but not much more than that. Used 'em to skip across Weaver's Pond. Worked better than any flat stones I ever found. Went six, seven skips at a time.

Ma tried to even get me to make a grilled cheese sandwich. At the time, my word hearing was not the best, and I was young enough to say I wanted a boy cheese sandwich rather than a girl cheese sandwich, heh, so she told me it was going to be a fried boy cheese sandwich. Now, peanut butter, I could do, with some grape jelly, or Ma's homemade pepper jam. You just took two pieces of bread and a knife and stuck what you wanted on the bread. Nothing to it. Course, the counter was frequently the worse for wear afterwards. But I could lift Bo up and he could lick that part off. But frying that cheese sandwich took a little more concentration, which I was never good at. One side or t'other, many times both, would come out too burnt to eat. Even Bo just sniffed at it and left it alone. And it wouldn't skip across the pond, either. I know, cause I tried.

The only other cooking I remember was when Sara and I made a cake for Ma and Pa's anniversary. It was supposed to be a surprise, so we couldn't ask Ma for help. As I said before, Sara was able to catch on to the cooking much better than I was, being as she was the oldest. She made the cake and measured out all the ingredients for the icing. I just got to stir everything and then lick the bowls. And then lay the icing on the cake. At least what was left of it. We put a little bit of lemon flavoring in it, and I'm afraid I got carried away with tasting the bowl just that little bit first. There wasn't too much left by the time the cake was cool enough to ice. Just enough to sort of write MA and PA across the top. They liked it anyway. At least they said they did."

Mom came into the room carrying a plate with two cookies on it, one for me and one for Uncle Albie. I guess they'd been cooking other things besides soup and biscuits. It looked and tasted like a sugar cookie to me, but Uncle Albie held his up and turned it over. "You didn't try to hide any raisins in there, did you?" He winked at me. "They're always trying to slip some fruit or vegetables in anything they can."

Mom pulled open the front door, she didn't dare touch the drapes, and peered outside. "Oh, my, look at that rain. I don't think we can make it to the car until this slows down some." She turned back to me. "Have you and Uncle Albie been getting along okay? I'm going to finish helping Mabel and Bertha clean up the kitchen, since we're going to be here for a while yet." It was still both Mabel and Bertha. There were times I wasn't sure she knew which was which.

Uncle Albie looked at the door, trying to listen to the rain behind it.

"I used to love the rain when I was a kid. Couldn't do any outside chores then, but I could still play in it. In a hard, steady rain, Sara and I would get down to our underclothes before Ma could say 'No!' or 'Wait till I find your swimsuits!', and we'd be out the back door with Bo, running and splashing through the backyard. Pa came out on the back porch under the overhang to sit and watch us. Ma yelled for him to watch for thunder or lightning, and to get us in right away. But Bo was better than Pa was at herding us inside if it got bad. We had races and threw some yard toys just to see how big a splash they'd make. The whole point was getting as wet as we could, and it not even being a bath night.

One time, though, it looked like it was never going to stop, raining and raining for what seemed like three to four days on end. We lived up on a little rise, just a mite above the other places, so we never got any water in the house, but some of our neighbors weren't so lucky. Old Miss Tucker's home got flooded on the ground floor, and she had to come over to stay with us. Course she brought a pie, cause she always had a pie or two, if she could keep them from being stolen. And, on the other side, the Cramers came sloshing over, with Joey and his sister, Lisa. And their dog, Pickles. Don't ask me where that name came from, but I suspect it filched a couple off the kitchen counter when they first got it.

It turned into a real party. The adults all talked and talked and played a lot of dominoes, even Miss Tucker. And us kids camped out in the parlor with blankets and pillows. Ma didn't even mind us making somewhat of a mess there, with our toys and running around. She just figured that was our special room for right now and it would all get sorted out when folks had gone home. Ma and Mrs. Cramer made a big pot of soup. I don't recall what kind, but I don't think I've had any better in my life.

That was the best rain, and we didn't care if it lasted forty days and forty nights, or not. This was adventure living."

Uncle Albie stretched and yawned. Mom came back in, pulling her jacket on, and holding mine out for me. "I think it's letting up a little, so we better make a run for it while we can. Say goodbye to Uncle Albie, and thank him for keeping you busy."

I got my coat on and zipped it up, then stepped over to Uncle Albie. He had his head on his chest and his eyes were closed. I was worried for a minute, then I heard a gentle snore. Then another.

"Goodbye, Uncle Albie," I whispered. "Thanks for all the stories. Hope to see you again soon." I could have swore I saw just the touch of a smile, but he wasn't about to let me know if he heard.

I WANT TO DANCE WITH YOU

I want to dance
To dance with you.
To be with you
Be entranced by you.
I want to dance
To dance with you.
To have a chance for romance with you.

I want to fly
To fly with you.
To soar with you
Come alive with you.
I want to fly
To fly with you.
To cry with you, fill the sky with you.

I want to share
To share with you.
Be here with you
And be there with you.
I want to share
To share with you.
To dare with you and to care with you.

I want to see,
To see with you.
The sun with you
And the sea with you.
I want to see
To see with you.
Be free with you and be me with you.

I want to dance
To dance with you.
To be with you
Be entranced by you.
I want to dance,
To dance with you.
To have a chance for romance with you.

If ... you feel like taking a walk with the family, be prepared for some sights or experiences that you weren't expecting. Just in case.

THE CAVE OF THE LOST SPIRITS

The Peterson family enjoyed family hikes. For Chuck and Joan, it was simply good exercise, enjoying nature and family time. For the boys – Tom, Rick, and Larry, ages ten to five – it was a socially appropriate way to spend their energy, running and climbing and yelling. The yelling may have disturbed the intended silence of the woods, but, hey, they were boys, and boys were going to yell, and why not do it in the great outdoors rather than in an enclosed space, like inside the house?

Chuck Peterson often said that, for Mother's Day, he took the boys hiking, and Joan would have the day to herself, and, for Father's Day, he took the boys hiking, and Joan would have the day to herself. Funny how that worked out.

But now, it was a crisp, sunny day in October, a week shy of Halloween, a perfect day for a walk. A long walk. All fall, the parents had been talking about a family hike in Lonely Hills State Park, and, in particular, to the well-known Cave of the Lost Spirits. But it was an hour and a half drive to the park, and that meant a full day dedicated to this adventure. Surprisingly, for once they now found themselves with a day with nothing planned, and impulsively said, "Let's do it."

Joan packed a picnic lunch and Chuck got out the hiking shoes, as well as a change of shoes for when the former inevitably got muddy, no matter the weather.

The boys behaved themselves on the ride, probably for two reasons. For the first one, they had all risen earlier than usual to get on the road, and the young ones were not quite fully awake yet. And the other reason was they had something specific to look forward to, to experience. The night before, Chuck had told them that the Cave of the Lost Spirits had some mysterious powers, something both scary and thrilling, something that they wouldn't discover until they got there. So, Tom and Rick talked about secret pirate treasure, or maybe ghosts, or perhaps hidden passages. The youngest, Larry, was getting anxious and told them to stop, but the two older ones didn't until Joan said it a little more forcefully. Then she glared at their father for a full minute for even suggesting anything.

Once they drove into the park, the parking lot was already about a third full, with a few families and several dogs climbing out of their cars. Chuck hoisted the backpack containing water and their lunch onto his back, and they followed another family, hoping those people knew where the trail started. Others were soon following them, so the Petersons guessed they were probably headed in the right direction.

It wasn't a very long hike, about 1 ¼ miles in along the bottom of a gorge, then slightly circling around to come back. After they entered the wooded path, though, the temperature seemed to drop about twenty degrees, and Joan stopped Chuck to break out the hats and gloves.

"It's a good thing I packed these."

"It's a good thing we're going to use them, as I would have hated to have carried them all the way in and all the way back out." Chuck always complained that Joan brought too much stuff whenever they went anywhere, but maybe this idea hadn't been too bad. He hated to admit that it was chillier than he had expected.

The other families had all moved on, and there was only an older man with a walking stick far ahead on the path. But now there was space for the boys to run on in front. "Stay in sight!", Joan yelled, but that means something different to sons than it does to mothers.

Chuck took a couple of pictures of the cliffs rimming the gorge, and, by the time the parents followed a curve in the path, the boys were nowhere to be seen.

"I can't see them. They went too far ahead." Joan raised her voice. "Boys, wait up!"

However, Chuck heard some giggling off to his left, and realized they were hiding behind a large stone. "I don't think they're that far ahead. I think we'll see them soon." He remembered having done the same thing to his parents when he was much younger. Running ahead, then trying to hide so he could come up behind them and scare them. For some reason, they never seemed to be that scared. He also heard some distant kids' voices, and those of a few anxious parents, so he realized they were not alone. They had gone about another twenty yards when he heard some scurrying and whispering behind them, but he resisted the urge to turn around.

Joan stopped to snap some of her own pictures of the morning sun making its way in flashes through the trees and off the cliffs. "This is spectacular here. I love how the sun comes through at this time of the day."

Chuck glimpsed the boys running through brush about twenty yards off the path now to the right, and heard Larry's voice crying, "Wait for me", followed by two loud "Shush"es. They disappeared around another rock further ahead.

"I'm kind of surprised the boys aren't climbing around all of these rocks. I would have been doing that as a kid."

"Well, there are a lot of signs saying, 'Don't climb the rocks! They are dangerous!'"

Chuck sighed. "I don't remember all these signs and fenced off areas when we were here, what, ten to twelve years ago."

"Before the boys, for sure. I think when we were still dating." She leaned over to him and kissed him. "It was so romantic then." However, the moment was soon gone, in a mist of motherly concern. She furrowed her brow and looked around. "Where are they?"

He pointed off to the right, up ahead. "They've been sort of circling us. I think they're over in that direction. They're okay. If something had happened, one of them would be yelling for us. Let them have fun exploring."

"Look, here's a plaque. Something besides warning us to stay off the rocks."

This section of the trail is dedicated to Owen Wolfe, a frequent hiker and supporter of the Lonely Woods State Park. He took a long walk one day and was never seen again. If you happen to come across him, tell him "Hey" from the rangers.

Chuck looked around him. "I still hear some voices, but I don't see anyone either ahead or behind. We must be in a sort of phantom zone, all by ourselves."

Joan grabbed his arm. "Come on, I want to catch up to the boys. I haven't seen them in a while. Are you sure they're ahead of us?"

After about another five minutes, with still no sign of their sons, they came upon an older man, sitting on a stone. He had on a heavier coat and a wool cap, holding onto a well-weathered walking stick, seemingly one he'd come across in the natural setting.

"Morning," Chuck called out. "Haven't seen anyone else in a little while."

The man smiled back. "Morning. It has gotten quiet along this trail."

"You didn't happen to notice three young kids go by here, did you?" Joan rubbed her hands.

"Three boys? About so high?" He gestured his hands in stairstep fashion to cover three different sizes.

She nodded eagerly.

"No."

Joan stared at him, while Chuck smiled beside her.

The man laughed. "I'm kidding. I'm sorry, I don't often get the chance to joke. They went by here a few moments ago. I suggested they should wait for their parents, but I don't think they heard me. Not the two oldest anyway. The littlest one stopped and pointed ahead, and said, 'We're trying to catch 'em,' then ran as fast as he could after the others. They're not far in front, but they seemed to think they were behind you. Sure they were yours?"

"Thank you." Chuck rolled his eyes. "Pretty sure they're ours. I think I can hear them yelling to each other again."

The man stood up. "Could I ask a favor? It's still a ways to where the creek is running, and I'm a mite thirsty. Would you happen to have any water you could share and maybe a bite of something? I hate to ask, but these old bones ain't what they used to be."

"Sure." Chuck shrugged off his backpack. "We've got a canteen, and maybe some paper cups ..."

"Oh, I've got one." He pulled an old tin cup off his belt. "Always carry one to dip out of the creek."

While he poured, Joan offered him a protein bar, full of nuts and fruit.

"Huh, haven't seen one of those before."

"Oh, it's just from the grocery store."

"Well, thank you kindly. I think this'll do me till I get where I'm going." He raised a hand and walked off in the direction from where they had come.

Chuck looked at Joan. "Huh, I don't recall passing a creek from that way. There's supposed to be one near the Cave, but not before. Just this dry riverbed we're following."

They both turned to watch the man, but the path was empty.

"What?" Joan cried out. "He was just here. He couldn't have gone that far that fast."

Chuck scanned the woods around them. "Maybe he went to relieve himself behind a tree. But, I still think we'd have seen him."

Joan was peering intently into the forest.

"Now, don't stare in case that is where he went." He put his arm around her. "Come on, I think we do need to find the boys."

They continued walking for a few more minutes, then heard the sound of kids coming their way.

"There they are." Chuck lifted his head.

But it turned out to be another young family returning from the direction of the Cave. A young boy and girl hopped ahead of their parents, but made sure to stay close.

"Hi, have you seen three young boys?" Joan asked, now with just a hint of apprehension.

The couple looked at each other, then shook their heads. The man answered, "There were several other kids at the Cave, but I don't recall a set of three boys. Sorry."

Chuck took Joan's arm. "They are probably hiding up there, waiting for us again. We'll find them." He looked back, watching the kids still skipping down the path. Ahead of them stood the older man, leaning on his stick and watching them.

Chuck pointed him out to his wife. "I guess that guy finally realized he was heading away from the water he wanted. Now he's coming back."

The other couple turned to face that way. "Who are you talking about?"

Chuck faced them. "That older man, in front of your kids. Right there." He turned back, but now there was no one but the children. "He was right there. Huh, he seems to have a habit of disappearing."

Joan grabbed his elbow. "Honey, we need to go find our kids." As they started to walk away, she shouted back, "Enjoy the rest of your day."

Now they walked a little quicker, with a little more urgency, a little more worry in their breathing. Joan called out the names, not concerned with disturbing the solitude anymore.

"Tom! Rick! Larry! You need to let us know where you are. You've gotten too far ahead. Tell us now!"

They stopped to listen, but there were no voices in return. Not even talking from ahead or behind. No tell-tale giggling or laughter.

"Chuck, Tom and Rick may try to keep up the hiding, but Larry would be calling out by now. He wouldn't want to be that separated from us." She yelled out again. "Boys, you have to come out, right now. I mean it."

Still no response.

Tom pulled out his map. "It looks like we're about ten minutes from the Cave of the Lost Spirits. Maybe they've gotten that far and are waiting for us there."

They hurried around a bend, and saw a figure briefly look in their direction, then turn and climb over a log, continuing on the trail.

"Hey!" Chuck called out, but the figure didn't stop. He said, "Isn't that the same guy again? How did he get in front of us?"

"I don't know. Come on, we need to get to that cave."

The path took a downward slope, and they had to slow to maintain their footing and not fall.

"Oh, I don't know if Larry could have handled this on his own." A touch of fear was entering Joan's voice.

"He's not lying along here, so he must have made it." Chuck almost said, "His body's not lying here," but stopped himself in time.

They came around a big rock and saw the Cave open up below them. It was a wide opening, but went deep enough that they could not see to the back of it. Just a darkness. Two women were attempting to gather four kids – three girls and one boy – telling them it was time to head back to the car and lunch. Their boys were not in sight.

They finished climbing down just as the others started back up.

"Excuse me, did you happen to see three young boys here?"

One of the women smiled at Joan. "No, just our kids. I know they make enough noise for a dozen, but we only saw one other family, and they headed back maybe twenty minutes ago."

Joan swiveled her head, hoping to spot some sign of her kids. Chuck said, "Thank you. Hope you have a good day."

After the others had gone far enough away to not hear them, he said, "Where is everybody else? There were quite a few people started this hike just ahead of us. There should be more people here."

"I don't care. I just want to find our kids. I don't care about anyone else."

She cupped her hands to her mouth. "Tom! Rick! Larry! Where are you?"

A voice came from behind them.

"Do you know the story behind the name of the cave?"

They turned to find the same older man. "I'm sorry, but I don't want to hear any story right now. My boys are missing." Joan was losing at her attempt to remain polite.

"Do you see those lights flickering on the back wall? Or at least as far back as you can see?"

Despite themselves, they faced the cave and noticed the lights for the first time. They seemed to be dancing and to be moving back and forth to a rhythm all their own. It did not seem to match the breeze or the movements of the surrounding trees.

"The story is that many years ago, a local tribe could not find a group of their children who had disappeared." Joan could not stifle a small gasp. "In looking for them, the searchers came across this cave and the flickering lights. While watching them, their children appeared from the back of the cave. The children reported that they had followed a figure into a small dark circle of trees and bushes and found themselves in the back of this cavern, talking with the spirits of their dead grandparents. After speaking with them for some time, the spirits guided them back to the open area where their parents were waiting. The elder members of the tribe searched the back of the cave, while the lights stopped flickering and appeared to simply watch them, but could not find any further holes or ways in. When they were done, the lights resumed their movements, and have done so to this day.

"Till now. Look."

The lights had stopped dancing. Tom, Rick, and Larry stepped out of the darkness. Larry called out, "Mom!" and ran to her. The lights started flickering again.

Joan hugged him tightly, then spoke, more to the older boys, "Where were you? We were worried."

Tom, out of breath, said, "We were running to catch up to you ..."

"You were ahead of us," Chuck interrupted.

Tom paused. "We were behind you. So we started running, but we couldn't see you. This man," he pointed to the older man, "told us to take a shortcut that went into the middle of a group of trees, and we ended up coming out here." Tom shrugged and Rick nodded. "I guess it was a shortcut."

Joan was crying by now. "Don't ever do that again."

Tom said in a small voice, "We're sorry." Rick nodded again.

The old man walked into the cave.

Chuck looked after him for a moment, then called. "Thank you, ... Owen." The man stopped and looked back. "The rangers say ... 'Hey!'."

"Tell them 'Hey' back." He turned and seemingly disappeared into the back wall.

Larry finally lifted his head away from his mother. "I'm hungry. Can we have lunch now?"

If ... you find yourself in a conversation with someone who seems a little beyond your usual circle of acquaintances, shall we say, would you continue talking with that person, or kind of move in another direction?

ALL OF US

The day started out, progressed through the middle, and actually was close to finishing off as more of the "same-old, same-old" (you know, that doesn't really look right in print – you hear it all the time, but rarely see it...).

Well, anyway, it had been more of the "same-old, same-old" (it looks better, maybe, just because I've now written it a couple of times). I teach seventh-graders and it was the day before Christmas break – they didn't want to be there and, to be honest, I was ready to call it a year. Some had finally turned in the paper that was due three days earlier, some still hadn't. Even though they had "promised" to get it done over the break, I wasn't going to hold my breath. Hope didn't spring nearly as much now as it used to.

I needed to finish my holiday shopping (okay, start it) and headed straight for the mall as soon as I could decently leave the school, also leaving a "promise" to myself to get those same papers graded and recorded.

The mall was full. Parking half-a-mile away was just the beginning. Jam-packed. Sardine-tinned. Bulging at the seams. Just what I expected ... and hated. I'd been hoping that, since it wasn't the weekend, it wouldn't be as bad, but I guess not-so-great minds think alike.

I had an aunt who wanted a scarf, a nephew who wanted a football, other family members who would get whatever I found for them, and a girlfriend who wanted a diamond. On a ring.

So, naturally, I first went to buy myself a pair of pants.

Now, there are dozens (probably hundreds, but I'm not going to count them) of women's clothing stores at any mall. And almost as many "young" shops – the kind of clothing that nobody over 21 can wear, and looks right only on ...I was going to say, on the models, but come to think of it, they're usually not wearing the clothes (or much of anything) on the posters or in the catalogues.

But men's clothing, if you're a male, has to be shopped for with a map, a compass, and a guide dog. Women can find the men's areas, because they know that the men's areas are where the women's areas are not.

Maybe I should have looked for the scarf first.

In the far corner of a department store, after forcing my way through the women shoppers (why are they all in the women's clothing sections when they're supposed to be shopping for other people?), and past the bored husbands trying to find a TV to watch a football game, I finally found a small section of men's pants. Now to find something that fits.

I don't like baggy – I look like I'm hiding my fat stomach. I don't like loose – I look like I'm hiding my fat rear. Even classic isn't what I remember as a normal fit. There were a couple that looked as unhip as I could find, so I grabbed them and went to stand in line for a dressing room. I was going to find out then and there if they fit, because I was not braving the maddening crowds again simply to return a pair of pants. I will already have to do that for the sweater another aunt will get me.

At the head of the line was a woman holding about a dozen slacks, and the three of us behind her soon found out why she was here.

"Harold, let me see those."

A man came out, apparently trying to hold his stomach in, looking un-happy and uncomfortable. "These are too tight."

"Well, you're going to have to lose a few pounds this year. They'll look fine then. Here, try this one now."

He took the new pair, gave us an "I'm sorry, but..." look, stopped hold-ing his breath, and let his stomach go. The snap popped, and he quickly backed up into the dressing room again.

Looking around, I realized there weren't any shorter lines in front of the other changing rooms, and they all seemed to have wives waiting to critique their husbands, anyway. I knew I should have looked for that scarf first.

A man stood about twenty feet away, in front of a mannequin wearing a three-piece suit. There was nothing unique about the guy. If I had been asked to describe him, I couldn't have said anything more than he was middle-aged (which covers a lot of ages), about average height, maybe the slightest bit overweight, with the slightest receding hairline.

But for some reason, I kept watching, and it took me a minute to figure out why.

The suit on the mannequin kept changing colors. Black, then tan, then gray. Then the vest was blue and the jacket gray, then the pants were gray and the jacket white. Then the vest was checked. Then the jacket was plaid. The man stood there, holding his chin with one hand and slightly shaking his head with each change.

I tapped the shoulder of the man in front of me.

"When did they make that display? That's kind of cool."

"What are you talking about?"

I pointed to the mannequin. "The suit that keeps changing. That's a pretty good idea for figuring out what goes with what, but I don't know how they do it."

"That gray suit over there?"

"No, the one that just went from dark green to light green." As a matter of fact, I didn't see any gray suit. "The one that man is looking at."

"That's a gray suit. It's been that way since I've been here."

Another shopper was passing by and I grabbed her arm. "Do you see that suit...now it's yellow..."

She pulled her arm away. "It's gray", and quickly moved in another direction.

The man in front of me looked at the suit, looked at me, shrugged his shoulders, then refocused on the dressing room door.

It was going to be awhile, and I wasn't getting anywhere in line, so I stepped out. The suit coat and pants were now purple, with the vest pink. The man turned as I approached and asked,

"Does that look right to you?"

"Well, I wouldn't wear it."

"That's what I was afraid of. Sometimes, things look so right in your imagination, but you have to actually see them in action. Then you realize it wasn't what you wanted at all."

"The suits are changing colors, aren't they? You see it?"

He seemed surprised at my questions. "Yes, that was my intention."

It was still purple and pink. It hadn't changed since I had started talking to him. "How do they do that?" I paused. "Wait a minute, you said 'my intention'. You're doing this? How do you do it?"

"I think of a color combination. And it happens."

It was now a grey coat with a black vest and pants. I thought of a light blue vest, but nothing happened.

"Oh. It's not going to happen for you ... unless you want me to do it." The vest turned light blue.

"How did you ...?" Too many variations on that question occurred to me, but one stood out. "How did you know what I was thinking?"

He turned to look straight at me.

"I think you and I need to have a talk." He took my arm and started to walk toward the exit.

"Hold on. Who are you? And how come no one else saw that suit changing colors?"

He held out his hand until I shook it. "At one time, my name was Stan Cooper, but there's no significance in that besides giving you something to call me. And, apparently, you needed to see that suit changing colors more than any of the others. Something different, ... instead of more of the 'same-old'?" Again, he turned to the exit.

I followed. What else was I going to do? You wouldn't be reading this if it was just about trying on pants.

Speaking of the pants, I realized I was still holding them as we neared the exit.

"Oh, I can't walk out with these."

He stopped and looked me right in the eye. A look that raised the hairs on the back of my neck, but all he said was, "You mean those?"

I looked down and found myself now carrying a bag with the pants inside.

"It's been taken care of. And, by the way," as we exited, "they do fit, about as well as anything else would have."

We headed toward a small coffee shop in between two youngish clothing stores, now with bored fathers instead of bored husbands. Typically, at a place like that during a season like this, there is absolutely no chance to get a table. People are about three deep around each one and there is always someone much faster or bigger than me, or more needy, if a spot does open up. But there was an open table, and, as Stan approached it and sat down, the sound of all the shoppers diminished, as if a window had been closed.

I looked at the line to order, then turned to ask him what he wanted, and if he really wanted to wait, but found two steaming cups sitting on the table.

"I like a simple hot cocoa," he pointed. "And this is your usual Irish Cream cappuccino. But non-fat. Just as good, trust me, but non-fat."

I sat. If you find a seat during the holiday shopping season, you sit.

"What's going on? You said we needed to talk." I took a sip, just the right temperature. And it was just as good.

"You wanted something different to happen. I wanted a conversation, with someone genuine."

"I'm someone genuine?"

"Let's just say, you are someone who doesn't have a specific agenda when talking with me, at least right now."

"Who are you?"

He laughed, but for the first time, I understood the concept of laughing with me, not at me. "So full of questions, but good ones. Legitimate ones. But we need to put aside right now who I am. That is what I want to find out from you.

"Which sounds even more confusing, I know." Stan shrugged. "I am asking you simply to accept it. In return, I will help you with your Christmas shopping."

For help with my Christmas shopping, I could accept a lot of things.

"All right." I could have sworn that I had already drunk about half my cappuccino, but the cup was still full. "What is it we need to talk about?"

"Well, first of all ...." He waved his arm toward the mall and the multitude of shoppers going by. "What do you see? I don't just mean the people passing the doorway. What is going on? What is happening here?"

I grimaced and took a moment to actually look at the scene. To try and see them as individuals, and not simply as a mass of humanity. The two women, I took them to be friends, smiling and laughing, enjoying each other's company as much as the shopping. The apparent father, with a list in one hand and two bags in the other, but taking time to wave when he saw someone he knew. Two teenaged boys, trying to look cool with their hands stuffed into their pockets, attempting to act nonchalant when teenaged girls walked past, yet widening their eyes and whispering to each other behind the girls. Wait a minute, I knew them. They had been in my class a few years ago. Even then, they had been observing the world out of sideways glances, interested and wanting to learn, but insistent on not letting anyone know.

"Well, they're shopping, but there's more to it than that. They're ... participating, being part of this Christmas experience. Yes, they are shopping, but, this time of year, it's more for someone else. They're actually paying more attention to the world around them. At least, that's what I'm seeing."

"Hmm." He took a sip from his still-full mug. "You may have a point. Maybe I have been missing something." He sighed and sat back. "It has been too long since I have seen the season. Not just the celebration of the birth of Christ, but the interaction, the joy of giving for the sake of others, the being together, the caring. So much has been obligation. You have to do this, you have to get that, church services have to be observed this way, parties have to be done at this time and in that way. Much of it is routine, and so much hustle and bustle. It has become something to be gotten over with rather than something to be anticipated." He took a much bigger drink. "And I have been so busy. I am so tired. So tired of all the questions and all the requests. Can't people just accept when good things are offered to them? Why do they look for more sinister meaning behind gifts that just make their lives better? And can't they make their own decisions based on what they already know they should do?"

I didn't have any answers for him, and, after what he had just said, I wasn't sure I was supposed to ask any questions. But after he was silent for a minute, I tentatively offered, "I think most people are trying to do their best."

Stan nodded. "I suspect you're right. In fact, I know you are right. Most people are doing their best. I guess the ones that should know better are taking up most of my time and energy." Now he shook his head. "So, what are you doing here?"

"Oh." It took me a couple of seconds to reorient myself to me. I found the list in my shirt pocket and pulled it out. "I need to get presents for a few people. Yet." I peered at him out of the corner of my eye. "Just to finish up, you know."

"No." He waved off the list. "I know you wait till the last minute to shop. Sort of your holiday tradition. At least that's what you tell yourself. I meant, why are you shopping at all? Why do you put yourself through this stress and the crowds? Aren't there other things you'd rather be doing? Like having dinner with Amy?"

"Well, I have presents to get yet. Like I said."

"I meant, why is it important to you to get them presents? Why does that matter so much to you? I know you rushed here right at the end of the school day to get it done."

"Well, because the people matter to me." I suddenly sat up and pointed a finger at him. "Wait a minute. You know I came from school; you know about Amy; you kept changing the colors of those clothes. In fact, I think your shirt is a different color from when I first saw you. Who are you, Stan Cooper? Are you Santa Claus? Or ..., I'm even more afraid to ask this, are you ... God?" I would have gulped, but, suddenly, I was having trouble swallowing.

"Does it have to be one or the other?" he gently asked.

Now I was having trouble breathing. I told myself, in, then had to tell myself, out, then repeat. A couple of times.

He chuckled, though I couldn't figure out what was funny. "You know, it has always struck me as odd that one of those concepts is considered a magical figure, and people consider the other a spiritual answer for everything. Both are regarded as benevolent and giving, wanting nothing in return. Except belief." He peered intently at me. "Or even a kind of belief. I'm not going to ask if you believe or not, that's your personal business. As I intended. Humans are supposed to make their own choices. I just want them to make the best decisions."

"Based on belief."

"Based on their genuine beliefs, not on what they think they're supposed to believe, or what other people tell them to believe."

I finally swallowed, but it was dry. Based on my beliefs at this very moment, I figured I no longer had any choices. "What do you want of me?"

He shrugged. "As I said before, a conversation." He stood up. "Why don't we take more of that walk?"

I looked down at my mug. It was still full, and I knew if I drank any more, I wouldn't be able to sleep at all that night. "Yeah, sure."

We exited the coffee shop and entered the flow of the crowds moving around the mall.

"You know ..." I wished he'd quit saying "you know", because I knew I didn't know. He knew. He knew everything.

"No, I don't know everything, But I do frequently have a good idea what you're thinking. What I was about to say was that I have trouble understanding why there is so much conflict between the different religions. They pretty much teach the same things – love one another, be kind to each other, appreciate the world – but they always want to emphasize the differences. Which are minor compared to what the primary message should be."

It took me a moment to realize that he was waiting for me to say something. Something that mattered. Something that had to be significant enough to justify him listening to me. I gulped. All I could do was speak from what I believed.

Before I could answer, a small child, maybe four or five, came whizzing by me, running as fast as his little legs could go, and much faster than I was certain I could run now. About twenty yards behind, his apparent mother was moving much slower, due in large part to the six bags she was carrying.

"Aloysius! You come back here right now! Aloysius!" If my mother had named me "Aloysius", I'd probably be running too, but that's being judgmental. In less frantic times, he may have just been called "Al".

I put down my bag, ready to run after him. However, before I could take a step, several others moved quickly in his direction. A woman wearing a hijab, a Muslim head scarf, had bent down in his path. She held out her arms, and he ran right into them. It was probably better that he had run into a strange woman than a strange man. She held him more gently than I would have and waited for the mother to catch up.

I couldn't hear the conversation, but the gratitude was obvious in the mother's face, and both women smiled. As did all the other people that had witnessed the attempted escape.

Thirty feet away, a large shopping bag being carried by an older man ripped, spilling out its contents on the ground. Three or four passersby stopped to help pick up the spilled contents, and one person transferred miscellaneous objects from one of their own bags into another, and offered him the empty one.

A bored husband was sitting on a nearby bench, but stood up and offered his seat to a middle-aged woman, who looked as if she needed a place to rest for a little while. She smiled and thanked him, gratefully taking the seat.

All of a sudden, it seemed as if a lot more people were smiling and laughing.

"I, I don't think it's a conflict between the religions." I took a deep breath. "I..." Maybe I was using "I" too much, but what the hell, I mean heck, dear God, I mean heck! "I believe it's more of a conflict between individuals who want to use religion to justify what they want to do. Or what they want other people to do. To make themselves feel better about what they do. Or want to do." I stopped and looked at Stan. "Does that make any sense?"

He stopped and cocked his head, as if considering my words.

I continued. "I..." Again with the personal pronoun. "I think that most people want to believe that they are doing and thinking the right things, but, maybe, sometimes, they are looking for confirmation not from ... God, or from their conscience, but from others who speak from a position of seeming power or knowledge, and simply sound like they know what they're talking about." I paused. "I'm rambling, I know, but you seemed to want to know what I thought." I stopped talking.

Stan smiled. "You're right. I wanted to hear what you had to say. Christmas is a time when people say what they think they're supposed to say, what others would approve hearing from them."

I felt encouraged to go on. "I'm afraid many people simply don't trust themselves, and when someone in authority offers them a shiny alternative that offsets what they fear, or somebody else to blame for what happens in the world, they are likely to grasp at it." I shrugged. "I'm probably wrong, or over-simplifying, but I think people would be better off doing the right thing because it's the right thing to do now, not because of what they'll get out of it. I think they are happier then." I gestured to the scenes in front of us.

He put his hand on my shoulder. "You are right. You are over-simplifying. But maybe the world needs more simplicity." He looked around at the crowds. "Or maybe faith. Not as in religion, but as in themselves, and in each other.

"Thank you. You have obviously thought more about these things than you were aware of. You have reminded me of my faith in the sincerity of your fellow human beings, even if they aren't always aware of it, themselves. Trust may be misplaced, but there is faith, and there is always hope."

He turned and walked away. As he was about to lose himself in the crowds, I called out, "You were going to help me with my shopping!" He reached a hand behind him and gestured at the ground.

Glancing down, I found four full shopping bags at my feet. I looked back up, but he was gone. I whispered, "Thank you."

Everything was already wrapped and labeled for the recipient. I guessed I was going to be as surprised as they were going to be when they opened the packages. There was even a small ring-sized box labeled, "To Amy, With all my love."

It looked like I was going to be acting on my beliefs, whether I had intended to or not.

ABOUT THE AUTHOR

After writing reports as a school psychologist for 42 years, Kevin Creager pursued a second career in writing what he wants to write. His first book, *We Cuss a Little: The Life and Times of a School Psychologist*, humorously, but honestly tells stories about his career. The second book, *The Body on the Roof*, is a small-town mystery relating the efforts of the local police to solve the death of a local teacher. His third book, *Time Out!*, is a humorous mystery wrapped in time travel and suspense.

OTHER TITLES BY KEVIN CREAGER

NOTE FROM KEVIN CREAGER

Word-of-mouth is crucial for any author to succeed. If you enjoyed *Dreaming Out Loud*, please leave a review online—anywhere you are able. Even if it's just a sentence or two. It would make all the difference and would be very much appreciated.

Thanks!
Kevin Creager

We hope you enjoyed reading this title from:

BLACK ROSE
writing™

www.blackrosewriting.com

Subscribe to our mailing list – *The Rosevine* – and receive **FREE** books, daily deals, and stay current with news about upcoming releases and our hottest authors.
Scan the QR code below to sign up.

Already a subscriber? Please accept a sincere thank you for being a fan of Black Rose Writing authors.

View other Black Rose Writing titles at
www.blackrosewriting.com/books and use promo code
PRINT to receive a **20% discount** when purchasing.

www.ingramcontent.com/pod-product-compliance
Lightning Source LLC
Chambersburg PA
CBHW051223210726
48290CB00003B/775